The Bones
of the Apostle

A Petrie and Pettigrew Novel

John Amos

RIVER GROVE
BOOKS

Published by River Grove Books
Austin, TX
www.rivergrovebooks.com

Distributed by River Grove Books

Design and composition by Greenleaf Book Group
Cover design by Greenleaf Book Group
Cover images used under license from ©Adobestock.com

Publisher's Cataloging-in-Publication data is available.

Print ISBN: 978-1-63299-901-6

eBook ISBN: 978-1-63299-902-3

First Edition

*To my wife, who has watched me type away for all hours and
still loves me. She sometimes interrupts my typing to ask,
"Do you love me?" And my answer is always "Yes."*

*To the detectives, real and fictional, who try to bring order to a chaotic
world. As Gilbert and Sullivan observed over a hundred years ago, "A
policeman's lot is not a happy one." That is as true today as it
was then. May your cases always be solved with elegance and dispatch.*

*To the Assyrians and Armenians who suffered through an enormous
calamity and still must live with its denial. May the world finally admit
the truth. You may have disappeared from history, but you have not
disappeared from our hearts. Your images will live on forever.*

*To those who survived the march into the desert.
May your souls find peace at last.*

*To the memory of Armin Wagner, a young German officer whose
conscience shamed us all and whose photographs have memorialized
the unthinkable. May your compassion forever uplift us,
and may your courage always give us hope.*

*And to everyone else who likes a good story. But remember,
while specific events may be fictional, the underlying reality is not.*

The Assyrian came down like a wolf on the fold,

And his cohorts were gleaming in purple and gold;

And the sheen of their spears was like stars on the sea,

When the blue wave rolls nightly on deep Galilee.

And there lay the rider distorted and pale,

With the dew on his brow and the rust on his mail:

And the tents were all silent, the banners alone,

The lances unlifted, the trumpet unblown.

And the widows of Ashur are loud in their wail.

—Lord Byron, "The Destruction of Sennacherib"

I should like to see any power in the world destroy this race,
this small tribe of unimportant people, whose history has ended.

—William Saroyan, "The Armenian and the Armenian"

Contents

Author's Note

This is only a story. As always, any brush with reality is purely coincidental. Any facts have been altered to suit the narrative. It is to be read for pleasure; it is not meant to instruct. It is written only to allow the imagination to roam freely unhampered by the cares of the world. For it is the imagination that makes us who we are and allows us to become something greater tomorrow than we are today.

Please enjoy the story.

Acknowledgments

I must always acknowledge Jane Friedman, whose hard-nosed advice about writing and publishing has inevitably been spot-on.

I owe a great debt to the editors of Greenleaf. Ava Coibion parsed every line and corrected my inelegance to make something readable. Adrianna Hernandez and Rebecca Logan shepherded the work through production with patience and wisdom. As always, any excellence is theirs; all mistakes are mine.

ONE

Tyger, Tyger, Burning Bright

Yellow eyes fixed on him. The tiger came out of the tall grass. The setting sun gleamed off its fearful stripes. It crouched lower into the grass, flattening itself for the spring. Its muscles coiled ever tighter. The tip of its tail slowed to a stop. A symmetry of death was a few feet from him. He could hear the grass growing in the stillness. He raised the barrel of his rifle: slowly, slowly, never losing eye contact.

Time stood still. The forest turned into night as he quietly cocked the rifle. The tiger's back rippled as it compressed for the spring. His finger tightened on the trigger.

Steady, steady, keep the sights on him.

The moment of truth had arrived.

"Flinders!" Pettigrew's voice shattered the tension. "Get your head out of that damn dreadful and help me move this piano."

His friend's outburst was immediately followed by a tremendous bumping and thumping.

Sounds like the walls are coming down.

"Yes, Thomas, I'm coming." Flinders turned off the reading lamp and the sitting room darkened. The Tiger faded into nothingness.

When Flinders arrived on the scene, he saw two very large draymen in dirty gray uniforms and slouched hats tugging a small piano up the front stairs. The keyboard twanged; the men huffed. Elise, a small figure in a dark dress, stood on the landing and directed them. The piano reached the landing, and Flinders and Pettigrew, along with Elise, pushed the spinet along the hall and into the spare bedroom. Sarah Bernhardt as Cleopatra smiled down from her playbill on the wall as the three struggled past. Flinders had purchased the playbill after seeing her perform at the Adelphi. "It is a reminder of our adventures in Egypt." He smiled at Sarah every day, and sometimes, when he was about to leave for the office, tipped his hat.

"I'm going to make this into a music room," Pettigrew announced. "Put it over there against the wall." He brushed a lock of blonde hair off his forehead and stood back to admire his acquisition. His blue eyes twinkled with delight.

Flinders opened the lid. "Where did you get this?"

"I saw it standing beside a shed in the London art market. It looked forlorn." Pettigrew loomed over the piano with a wistful expression.

"Forlorn?" Flinders inspected the piano's dusty top. There were fine scratches all along it. Flinders ran his finger along the worn keyboard lid. "Forlorn, indeed."

Elise paid the draymen; they touched their caps and left.

"It called to me."

"Naturally." Flinders grinned. "It recognized another forlorn soul."

"You talk too much, especially in this moment of great artistic promise." Pettigrew adjusted the piano bench.

"I am going to take music lessons." Pettigrew widened his eyes like an owl. "My muse has been awakened."

"Your muse . . ." Flinders paused. "I'm not sure whether I should laugh or cry."

"What do you mean?"

"I mean that we have suppressed our softer side for so many years, and now it comes out like a bubbling spring." He opened the keyboard and sat down. "But in your case, it's more like a canal."

He played a couple of notes.

"It needs tuning. I have sent for a piano tuner."

"Music lessons?" Flinders shook his head. "And you want to turn this room into a den of musicians. I suppose busts of Beethoven and Wagner will be scattered about, and portraits of Liszt and Chopin will glower from the walls." Flinders leaned into the piano and played a scale. "But why the piano? Why not the zither?"

"Nonsense. I am not Austrian."

"I was only inquiring into your thought process."

"I thought of taking up the trumpet and playing trumpet voluntaries."

"Trumpet voluntaries?" Flinders grinned. "I am astonished. You wanted to become a Baroque musician?"

"Yes, the ringing notes of the trumpet are like cascades of golden metal rippling down a long waterfall."

"Cascades of golden metal, is it?" Flinders let his jaw drop in exaggerated shock. "I now have a modern-day Shelley on my hands. Well, what happened? I see a piano, not a trumpet."

"I'm very fond of Handel." Pettigrew sighed, stepping closer to the piano and resting his hand on it. "But the trumpet was too difficult to play."

"Handel?"

"Yes, Handel."

"Wait! I can see it now." Flinders put his hands over his eyes. "You could wear a huge curled wig, sneak up on a miscreant, and subdue him with a trumpet blast." He crept around the room like a cat stalking an imaginary mouse. "We could have run ads in all the London papers with a picture of you in a wig."

"A wig, you say?" Pettigrew's eyes sparkled with amusement. "I've always fancied myself wearing a great wig." Pettigrew fingered his mustache. "It would go beautifully with my mustache."

"No, it wouldn't." Flinders made a face. "The wig is white, and your mustache is blonde. Besides, Handel did not have a mustache."

"We all have to modernize."

"Just think of the caption," Flinders went on. "'A blast from the past saves your cash.' Too bad you couldn't learn to play the trumpet."

"A huge wig with curls down to my shoulders." Pettigrew stroked an imaginary wig. "I could look like the Lord Chancellor, himself."

"Indeed, you could." Flinders bowed. "But, alas, you have abandoned the trumpet."

"Never mind that." Pettigrew dusted the piano. "I decided on the piano. Myra Hess is going to give me lessons. We have already begun, and she is teaching me to play." He pulled a sheaf of sheet music from a battered satchel.

"What have you got there?"

"Mozart."

"Mozart?"

Pettigrew placed the music on the piano and stood back in admiration.

"Looks like a lot of notes—are you sure that you can play them?"

"Mozart cut his notes down after the emperor complained about the notes."

"Well?" Flinders asked. "Well?"

"Well, nothing. It is 'Twinkle, Twinkle, Little Star,' and it is really quite lovely."

"How did you manage that? She is a famous pianist." Flinders was surprised. He fingered the keys. "She gives concerts all over the world.

Somehow, I can't imagine this great lady playing 'Twinkle, Twinkle, Little Star' with you."

Pettigrew arched a sly smile. "You underestimate my charm."

"I'm not sure the world is ready for this." Flinders grinned. "Next you'll be wanting to debut at Royal Albert Hall." He thought for a moment. "Wait! The vision comes to me." He placed a finger to his lips and lowered his voice. "The house lights dim. You step onto the stage, your studs flash, your cuffs gleam, you brush your tails aside and sit down at the piano. You open the music and place your hands gently on the keyboard. The audience holds its breath in anticipation."

His voice trailed off into a hush.

"And?"

"And . . ." Flinders grinned. "'Twinkle, Twinkle, Little Star.'"

Pettigrew sniffed. "For a supposed classical scholar, you have no sense of the finer things in life." He sat down at the keyboard and played scales.

Flinders walked back down the hall to the sitting room. Sarah Bernhardt smiled down at him as he passed her playbill. He looked up at her dancing eyes.

"Not a word, you hear," he told her, putting his finger to his lips.

He returned to the sitting room and poured himself a glass of wine. He stood for a moment in the darkened room and held the glass up. Medusa stared at him, her eyes glowing yellow streetlight from the windows. He swirled the claret around in the wine glass and examined its stem with her face on it. She looked back at him through curly locks. Her face was pointed, and her chin was narrow. Her eyes were wide open and unblinking; they fixed Flinders with an unspoken question.

"What will you do next?"

A good question, Flinders thought. *A good question indeed.* He peered into the glass and contemplated the wine. *What was it that Kudret once said? A glass of wine is like a tulip, red on the outside and dark in the center.* Flinders moved to the window and stared out through the white curtains. Nothing moved in the street below except an occasional cab. The tinkle of piano notes came from the bedroom. *What is out there?* He pulled the curtains wide. *Kudret pined for a lost empire, a past that was drifting away from him. Do I pine for a lost world as well?*

He closed the curtains.

I drink too much.

He turned and sat down. He crossed his legs and carefully pulled his trouser leg up at the knee to prevent wrinkles.

The sitting room was warm. Flinders unbuttoned his collar; the wine relaxed him. *And now I sit comfortably and listen to Thomas play his piano. Elise sings downstairs and her cooking warms my nose. My life should be full and content. But why am I not content?* He twirled the glass and saw Pettigrew return from the bedroom through its crystal stem. Pettigrew settled himself into a leopard-skin chair and stretched his legs out. He opened the evening paper and read aloud the headlines, PARLIAMENT APPROVES OLD AGE PENSIONS.

How appropriate, thought Flinders. *We can all become pensioners.* Cleopatra looked down from her wall, her dark eyes brooding. The smell of cooking mutton wafted up from the kitchen. Occasional traffic rumbled in the street below.

"Thomas, do you think that we should become pensioners?"

I can hear the mites moving in the carpet, Flinders thought. *I wonder what it would be like to be a mite. Perhaps if I become a pensioner I could converse with the mites.*

"Flinders, we have an excellent retirement program at the office."

"Thomas, I know about that, but should we retire?"

"Do you want to retire?"

"No."

"Then you have your answer."

"Old age pensions, indeed," Flinders said and took another sip of the wine. "Thomas, I'm bored. We need some excitement." He put his glass down and turned back from the window. "We haven't done anything in years. We've been too caught up in running this detective agency. How many employees have we got? Ten? Twenty? They all look alike, and they are all as bland as can be." He shook his head. "They come up to me and ask inane questions. The other day, one of them came flying out of the loo and nearly knocked me over. He wanted to know what he should do if a robber attacked him with a knife."

"Well," Pettigrew said, looking up from his paper. "What did you say?"

"I said, 'Shoot him.'" Flinders shook his head in disgust. "'Suppose it was only a small knife,' the nitwit said." Flinders laughed. "Shoot him anyway, right?"

"Quite right, indeed."

Flinders turned back to the window. "Sometimes when I go to the office, I think I am in the London fish market, with all those staring eyes." He laughed. "It's like walking through a school of trout."

"You said that before, I believe." Pettigrew rattled his paper. "They do all look alike. But there were a few that had some promise."

"You mean the Americans?" Flinders said.

"Yes, one American was most interesting. I think his name was Marlow," Pettigrew said. "He was very tall and very young. He only stayed a few months and then went back to America. I played chess with him once. He drank American bourbon all the while."

Flinders parted the curtains. The hum of traffic floated up from the street; fingers of light slanted through the window and crept across the green carpet. A statue of Isis turned from white to pink on her pedestal. Her smile slowly faded in the gloom.

The silence deepened.

Pettigrew turned on the glass sconces. "We are the only ones left. The era of great detectives is gone. Now there is no one left but men named after garden tools."

"That would be Mr. Spade, another American," Flinders said, nodding. "I received a letter from him the other day. He is young and just getting started."

"There was one more American as well." Pettigrew set his paper down on the small table beside his chair. "Yes, I remember him. A fellow from Boston, 'Blackie' or something like that—a stylish man. But none of these newcomers have the elegance that Holmes had."

"Elegance." Flinders nodded. "That is their problem; they have no panache."

"Panache, indeed." Pettigrew smiled. "Panache is the mark of a great detective."

"Do we have panache, Thomas?"

"Indeed we do, Flinders."

"I miss Holmes." Flinders sighed. "His savoir-faire set the standard for detectives."

"And I miss him as well."

"Thomas, did I ever tell you about the time Holmes and I went to pubs?"

Pettigrew shook his head. "About a hundred times, I think."

Flinders laughed. "We met in the street. I was disguised as a pensioner; he was disguised as an old woman. But his elbows were wrong. You cannot disguise elbows, and he should have covered them. I said, 'Mr. Holmes, I presume?' He jumped and looked, and then he laughed and said, 'Good show, young man, but your walk is off.' He saw right through my costume." Flinders refilled his glass. "One thing led to another. We made a bet to see who could create the most believable disguise. We went off to pubs to see if anyone would recognize us."

"You came home smelling of beer." Pettigrew chuckled. "Cheap beer at that."

Flinders sat down in a zebra-striped chair. "I never could get the best of him. Once, he disguised himself as an aging prizefighter from Manchester." He laughed at the memory. "Holmes was a tall man, but in that disguise, he looked barely five feet in height, and I could not understand him because his accent was so thick."

"What happened?"

"I said, 'Mr. Holmes, I presume?' He replied. 'Gar, you got me, mate.' I told him that was because his eyes were wrong. A prizefighter's right eye should have the scars from straight left jabs, but his left eye showed all the scar tissue. He grinned and told me, 'You're right, young man. I did this disguise looking in the mirror, and of course it is backwards.' He said something like, 'Well done, we'll make a detective of you yet.' Then we went to a pub." Flinders toasted with his glass and laughed. "He had the fastest elbow in all of London. After a couple of pints, he would tell fantastic stories." He leaned forward. "You know, he was far more personable than Watson lets on."

Pettigrew frowned. "I thought Watson said that Holmes didn't drink."

"Watson was a stodgy old devil—he made Holmes appear stiff and sour."

"I don't think Watson ever recovered from his wound in Afghanistan."

"That may be."

"So now I will tell you a Holmes joke," Pettigrew said, spreading out his hands.

Flinders groaned. "Please spare me—not the tent joke again."

"Remember the case of the *Giant Rat of Sumatra*?" Pettigrew paused dramatically.

"I quiver with anticipation."

"Well, Holmes and Watson were following the rat along a path of blood-stained rocks. Holmes picked up a rock and said, 'Watson, look at this.' Watson asked Holmes, 'What is this rock?' Holmes replied, 'Sedimentary, my dear Watson, sedimentary.'"

Flinders laughed. "That is much better than your tent joke."

Then both sat in silence. A cab in the street outside backfired. The clock ticked loudly in the dining room, and the air in the sitting room was heavy.

Finally, Flinders spoke. "The old days are gone," he said. "Thomas, our souls are at risk." He waved his glass, almost spilling the wine. "We did not become detectives to be humdrum businessmen. Remember when those harem guards attacked us? That was the life."

"Harem guards, is it? You were lucky that you did not get sliced by a scimitar."

"Nonsense. I had everything under control."

"Yes, and you looked wonderful in your costume." Pettigrew picked up his paper and folded it. "I particularly liked your earrings. They were wonderful."

Flinders grinned. "And so was my poetry."

"You cribbed it from Cyrano."

"Cyrano was the greatest swordsman in the world."

"But, as I remember . . ." Pettigrew set the paper down, its pages in a jumble, and filled a glass of wine for himself. "There was an Assyrian woman who said something about clogs." He scratched his head. "Yes, I have it. She wanted to know if you were man enough to wear clogs like the sultan did when he entered his harem."

"The clogs. . . . Yes, I remember what she said." Flinders paused and stared at Medusa.

"She had gray eyes, and you were quite entranced with her."

"She had gray eyes." Flinders lowered the glass and turned to the window as though searching for a lost memory.

Then he saluted with his glass. "A remarkable woman." He looked into the depths of the wine. "Yes, I wonder where she is." He swirled the glass. "Thomas, sometimes when I wake up at night, I can see the gray eyes watching me."

Would I wear clogs before her?

Pettigrew posed an evil grin. "Her question, however, has still remained unanswered."

"Never mind the clogs."

Dishes rattled up from the kitchen below. A dog barked somewhere outside. Cleopatra's eyes glowed in the dim light. Flinders stared up at her dark eyes.

She calls to me across the centuries.

Would I also wear clogs before her?

Flinders swirled his wine and stared at it. "Thomas, the far pavilions call me."

"The far pavilions, is it?" Pettigrew set his wine down and picked up the latest popular novel, *Of Human Bondage*. "I've been reading this," he said. He studied the book. "This fellow, Maugham, is terribly depressing. I do not understand how anybody can read his books." He closed the book.

They looked at each other. Yellow streetlight from the window played across Pettigrew's face. Flinders looked at Cleopatra and then at the window, unable to express his yearning.

Finally, Pettigrew spoke. "So, you want action, do you? You want to travel around to godforsaken places and be shot at by unfriendly people? But you may be right." He refilled his glass. "Perhaps we could use one last adventure. That would be much better than reading dreary novels."

"Indeed, it would."

"One for the road, you might say."

"One for the road, indeed."

Flinders felt the sitting room grow still. Cleopatra pouted; Isis opened her eyes wide. Puffy birds circled the dining room. Dishes rattled in the kitchen. The windows slowly went dark. A church clock boomed the hour. The clock in the dining room echoed it in shimmering notes.

And so it was, thought Flinders. *Two men with a yearning for adventure. Our bodies have aged, but our youthful wanderlust has not lessened over the years.*

The booms faded into silence; the chimes tapered off. But the wanderlust remained, bubbling in him like a glass of sparkling champagne.

"Yes, once more to the horizons beyond the horizon." Flinders held his glass high. "To the horizons forever lost."

"To the horizons beyond the horizon." Pettigrew repeated, raising his own glass. "To the horizons forever lost." He took a sip. "I'll drink to that."

Their glasses clinked.

"Speaking of adventure," Flinders said, "have we heard from Lawrence lately?"

"Yes, he wrote a note the other day," Pettigrew answered. "He's in Cairo. He writes that he has been recruited by Naval Intelligence to gin up some sort of revolt in the Arabian Peninsula. He thinks that it will be more exciting than wandering around Crusader castles."

"Really?" Flinders laughed. "Now that is an adventure for you."

"I have never liked camels, as you well know." Pettigrew sniffed disdainfully. "I prefer my adventures to be in big cities, and not in sandy tents."

"I thought you liked Nellie?"

"Nellie was not a camel—she was a friend."

"She almost gave her life for you."

"Indeed, she did." Pettigrew stared into space. "Whoever thought an animal would care so much."

"Perhaps she saw something in you."

"Do you think so?"

"Of course, or she just might have been nearsighted."

"I will ignore that."

Flinders sighed. "I will have to admit that was an adventure par excellence. But will we ever have another?"

"Time is not on our side, my friend."

"I wonder about that." Flinders stared at his glass. "Perhaps it is, more than we believe." Then held it up to the light. "Yes, another adventure is just what's called for."

"We shall have to wait on the times." Pettigrew's blue eyes turned dark. "Remember, my friend, what that Sufi fellow once said, a long time ago? You should learn from his wisdom." He closed his eyes and remained silent for a moment. "It comes to me now:

> *Patience is not sitting and waiting,*
> *It is foreseeing. It is looking at the*
> *Thorn and seeing the Rose, looking*
> *At the night and seeing the day."*

When Pettigrew finished reciting, Flinders grinned. "Did Gertrude read you that? That sounds like her."

"Ah, yes, Gertrude of the green eyes. I do read, you know." Pettigrew sniffed. "And I am quite taken with Rumi's poetry."

"Nonsense." Flinders shook his head. "We are not Sufis, and you are not Rumi."

"Patience, my friend, patience." Pettigrew closed the book and looked thoughtful. "But you are right—when we were at Carchemish, Gertrude read me Sufi poetry. She had translated most of Hafiz and Rumi." Pettigrew put his book down and sighed. "Gertrude was a remarkable woman. Those green eyes. Sometimes, Flinders, I miss the desert at Carchemish. Lawrence may have been right when he said, 'The desert is clean.'"

"I am not sure that he was talking about the desert."

Soft rain tapped on the windows. Flinders clicked on the glass table lamp. Light from the bulbs cascaded off its crystal facets. "Eloquent, indeed, my dear fellow," he said. "But since when did you become a Sufi poet? Ah, yes, you and Miss Bell. And the dark-eyed Unayza. How could I not remember? You should have taken the shaykh's offer. Just think, 'ten strong sons and daughters without number.'" He paused. "Although, I do not think the world is ready for ten more Pettigrews." He laughed. "Still, the thought of a line of Pettigrews marching across the desert is intriguing."

"Wait! I have it: a movie about the desert." He continued as he whirled around the sitting room. "Think of it: a silent about you striding about in long robes, dazzling beautiful maidens, and fighting camel duels in the sunset. I hear the Americans are going to make such a movie—they are thinking about using some young Italian who dances tango at a restaurant. Rudolph something or other, but they should cast you, mighty 'Abul hol,' instead."

"And I suppose that you would play a shaykh dressed in white and dance the tango."

"That has possibilities," Flinders said. "I could wear a broad hat and crack a whip."

"Shaykhs don't wear broad hats and crack whips."

"Details," Flinders scoffed. "You are always into details. It is the action that counts."

"No doubt that vamp woman you got drunk would play opposite you." Pettigrew closed his eyes. "Now, what was her name? Theda, I think."

"Ah, yes, Theda of the smoldering eyes." Flinders chuckled. "But we are talking about adventure. Thomas, don't you miss the desert and the action? Remember how you fought the Bulbul?"

"But Flinders, that Bulbul fellow almost killed me."

Flinders frowned. "I know, I was there." He put his glass down. "I saw women come out of the tents and spread out behind you. They held their children in their arms and cried out for the great warrior. Their warbling echoed off the hills." Flinders widened his eyes to convey the excitement that the words did not truly express. "I have never heard such a sound. It was terrible in its intensity."

Pettigrew nodded.

"The sound grew and grew until the entire desert vibrated to its rhythm."

"I heard it as I rode out to meet him."

"You do not know." Flinders covered his eyes for dramatic effect.

"The men kissed their wives and children goodbye. The shaykh gave the order to advance. 'We must meet them as men.' His blade flashed in the setting sun. 'Allahu Akbar! Allahu Akbar!' the riders shouted. The camels rolled forward. I could see the green flags fluttering over their heads. Lawrence handed me a pair of machine pistols and shouted, 'We will die like the men we are.' And Thomas, we were prepared to die."

"Go on," Pettigrew said flatly.

He does not respond. Does he not wish to remember?

Seeing that his efforts were having no effect, he tried again. "And then *nothing*. The line of camels disappeared." Flinders shook his head. "Sunlight faded into night. In the morning, we searched for you. We found you lying with your arm around Nellie's neck. She was covered with bites. There was blood all around. The Bulbul was dead next to you. His mouth was wide open; he had no teeth. We took you back. The women laughed and cried. The men put down their swords and embraced their wives and children. The camp resounded with tears and laughter. 'Abul hol has defeated the jinn. Abul hol has defeated the jinn.' The shaykh knelt down before you."

Pettigrew raised an eyebrow—the last bit seemed to have piqued his interest. "Go on," he said.

"The men carried you. The boys chanted, 'Ya, ya, Abul hol, ya, ya, Abul hol,' and the women crowded around you. Everyone laughed and sang. I asked Lawrence what they were singing, and he translated. 'The great warrior has returned victorious. The giant with hair the color of lemons in the sun has saved us. We are alive. Rejoice, rejoice in the will of God.' You were half conscious. You do not know what you did." Flinders gave Pettigrew a serious look. "Unayza never left you."

"I did not know."

Flinders paused. "But Thomas, there is something else."

Pettigrew looked up. "Something else?"

Flinders hesitated. "Thomas, something I never told you."

"Yes?"

"I tried, once before, but I could not, you were so happy to be home again."

"What is it?"

"While you were still recovering, Lawrence came to me. He was worried."

"About what?"

"He said. 'One night, I was walking outside the shaykh's tent, and I saw Unayza go in. I stopped; I could hear them arguing. The shaykh said, 'You must stop tending Pettigrew—the elders are grumbling.' She said, 'Father, I love him. I will not leave him.' The shaykh told her that the elders would demand that she be stoned to death. She shouted, 'Father, I carry his seed within me.'"

"She said *what?*"

"She said, 'Father, I carry his seed within me.'"

"She was *with child?*" Pettigrew bent over as though he had received a heavy blow. His wine spilled on the carpet. "Flinders, help me," Pettigrew cried. "She was hard as the desert and soft as a rose." He rocked back and forth in his chair. "I left her alone when she needed me the most." He put his hands over his face. "I will never be forgiven for this." He looked up at Flinders. "Unayza, Unayza, what have I done?"

Now that the story had begun to come out of him, Flinders could not stop. "The tent flap opened, and she rushed out. She was crying. I went in. The shaykh was sitting with his head in his hands. He looked up. His eyes were wide with grief. 'Aurens, what can I do? She will die in the desert.' I touched his shoulder and told him that God would find a way. He looked down. 'Yes, God will find a way. I must pray.'"

"You're sure of this?" Pettigrew covered his face. "I walked away from her world, but her world now pulls me back into it."

"Yes." Flinders filled another glass.

The sitting room was breathless as they stared at each other. Rain drummed louder on the window. Flinders watched the yellow light from the street below filter across Pettigrew's strained face. It was the face of a man who had just seen a ghost.

"She was with child?" Pettigrew's eyes opened wide. His jaw quivered.

"I do not know. That was what she said."

"What have I done?" Pettigrew's face crumpled. "Where is she?" He put his face in his hands. Flinders saw tears trickling down his cheeks. Unable to watch, he turned away.

"I must find her." Pettigrew rocked in his chair. His wine spilled again, a slow circle of red despair.

"You cannot find her any more than I could help a small baby with a twisted lip."

His face was red, and he murmured against my chest.

"And *so*, you want more?" Pettigrew raised his voice. "You want more blood and action? You want more death and destruction? You were almost killed in Alexandria yourself—was not that enough?"

"Inji saved me." Flinders closed his eyes as the memory of the saw teeth flooded his mind. *The garrote closed ever tighter. The sawtooth wire cut into my neck. Suddenly, the garrote loosened. I saw her standing over me; she had a knife in her hand.* "She killed the cultist and gave me an antidote to the poison."

"Didn't you ever wonder why she just happened to have an antidote?"

"We will never know who she was."

Pettigrew stared at the red circle in front of his chair. "There may be no Injis around to save you next time."

"Thomas, we are condemned," Flinders said.

Pettigrew shook his head. "Even condemned men get reprieves."

Flinders stood up and walked to the window. He looked at the wet street below, but his eyes did not see the slick cobbles. "There is something out there—I can sense it." He turned to Pettigrew. "There is something out there, like the tiger in the dreadful."

"Your tiger doesn't exist," Pettigrew said. "You have invented it in your imagination."

"No, its ferocity is real. It consumes me."

"You will never meet it."

"I must."

Pettigrew refilled his glass and held it up in the waning light. Medusa peered from its stem. "What you want is too much for a man."

"It is never enough."

"Flinders, you can never defeat your tiger."

"I must defeat it," Flinders said. "The yellow eyes glow. My saber must meet them."

"Flinders, Flinders. What can I do with you?"

"Thomas, our time is out of joint."

"The far pavilions?"

"Yes."

"Always the far pavilions?" Pettigrew questioned.

"Always the far pavilions." Flinders's voice was firm.

"We may die searching for the far pavilions."

"So be it."

Pettigrew swirled the wine. "Sometimes, in the late evening, when I'm about to fall asleep, I see ghosts of faces and hear distant voices." He took a long drink. "You may be right." He rubbed his chin. "Yes, you may be right."

He sees ghosts of faces and hears distant voices, and so do I, thought Flinders. "Thomas, we are condemned to return. There is a legend."

"So now you are the new Herodotus?"

"Herodotus spoke only of the Nile," Flinders said. "We are condemned to a worse fate."

Pettigrew scowled, his lips twisting as if he had tasted something bitter. "The jinn, you mean."

"Yes, the jinn."

Pettigrew sipped the wine. "You think the desert calls us?"

"Not just the desert."

The rattle of dishes drifted up from the kitchen below. Isis smiled

from her pedestal. A car honked outside. The sitting room was expect-
ant with an unanswered question. Flinders stared at his glass. The wine
was red with a dark center. *Like one of Kudret's tulips.* "What is it about
the unknown that calls to me?" A poem ran through Flinders's mind,
something by William Blake. *A strange man with wild eyes, eyes that
burned, like the tiger he described.*

> *Tyger Tyger, burning bright,*
> *In the forests of the night;*
> *What immortal hand or eye,*
> *Could frame thy fearful symmetry?*

Is this tiger somewhere in a distant forest, or is it within me?

Flinders went to the window, thinking he heard the arrival of the
delivery men. There they were down below, dressed in baggy brown
trousers and removing a carefully wrapped sofa from the back of a
lorry. "At last, Thomas—this may be my greatest decorating moment."

Pettigrew covered his eyes. "Perhaps we should petition Parliament
to declare a national holiday."

"You have the soul of a turnip."

"Broiled and buttered, I hope."

Flinders rushed downstairs. "No, no, Elise—I'll let them in."

When Flinders thought about it, their life had become comfort-
able. Their reputations—and income—had grown over the years, and
their two-man firm had grown in size accordingly. Even so, they had
remained in the flat where it all started. Over time, Flinders had the
flat redecorated; the ornate Napoleon III furniture had been replaced
by sensuous art deco sofas and chairs. The silk and gold had become
ivory and ebony. Leopard skin and zebra stripes had replaced ornate,

Baroque patterns. The Sultanabad rug had evolved into a floral Chinese deco carpet.

"Yes, yes," Flinders exclaimed as the tradesmen arranged the most recent purchase, a small sofa. "Art deco is the wave of the future."

Pettigrew surveyed the new furniture. "I rather liked the old gilt stuff."

"Thomas, you are so out of date that even Pliny couldn't find you."

"Pliny, is it?" Pettigrew felt the springs of a leopard skin chair. "I doubt that even Pliny would approve this."

The delivery men brought the carpet up next. "Thomas," Flinders said, "this is a genuine Nichols rug. It is just like the one in that Erté fellow's apartment in Paris."

"You mean that Russian fellow?"

"Indeed so."

"Maybe you should move to Paris." Pettigrew looked unimpressed. "You should have taken up decorating. Every time I turn round, you are bringing in something new."

"We must keep up with fashion," Flinders said. "How many times have I told you that fashion makes the man?" He paused. "Or in your case, the Pettigrew. Although that may be an impossible dream."

Pettigrew shook his head. "I think I need a cigar."

"Good. Please go outside and talk to the sphinx, while we improve things up here."

Even the hallway was changed. The dark red Afghan rug was replaced by a blue silk Chinese carpet. Sarah Bernhardt now smiled down at a golden tiger striding among pink blossoms.

"More energy," Flinders said.

Some things remained unchanged. The oil painting of Cleopatra remained over the fireplace, and the statue of Isis remained on its pedestal. The garden with its small sphinx was untouched. And the garden still smelled of roses. Flinders now spent much more time in it. He had taken up tending the roses and filled the flat with bouquets. It gave him immense pleasure to do so. "Thomas, roses are the queens of the flower kingdom." He waved a huge white rose with a pink center under Pettigrew's nose. "Smell this. This is Souvenir de Malmaison and it is over a hundred years old. Empress Josephine loved it."

Pettigrew sniffed. "Quite nice."

"I grew it myself from a small cutting—it is beside the sphinx. Think Thomas, what you smell is what Empress Josephine smelled. The past has come alive in this rose." Flinders sniffed the rose, and his imagination wandered. *The chateau was a dark mass at the end of the pebbled drive. The morning sun crept over the hill behind it. She walked among the roses, their leaves wet with dew. She bent over a large cream rose with a pink center. She lifted it to her nose. The sun burst across the horizon. Its heat warmed the roses. She stood in the light and the fragrance, a white silhouette in a sea of pink and red.*

"So now you have become the new Napoleon?" Pettigrew scratched his nose with the edge of his paper. "Perhaps we can find you a large, cocked hat."

"You don't understand—this is history."

"It's a rose."

"You are a stump," Flinders said, shaking his head and putting the roses in a large vase.

He joined the Royal Horticultural Society. When he returned from one of the meetings, Pettigrew observed him with amusement on his face. "I just can't imagine you sitting around discussing flowers with a group of elderly ladies," he said.

"You have no soul." Flinders smiled. *Thomas, you are as solid as a rock, but you miss the joys of life—the flowers have become such a big part of my world.*

"Do you intend to take up beekeeping as well, like Holmes?"

"I once said that you had the imagination of a trout. I take that back—you have the imagination of a flea."

"Fleas are the salt of the earth."

Early one morning several weeks later, Flinders rushed up the back stairs, a tiny bird in his hands. "Look what I found. It's a baby finch. It's beautiful."

"A bird?" Pettigrew looked up from his paper. "What are you going to do with it?"

"Put it back in its nest, of course. But I wanted you to see it. So small, so lovely."

"Ah, yes." Pettigrew looked at the bird. "I remember when you held real babies once." He smiled. "I must say, I was proud of you then. I think that there is a side to you that you have carefully hidden all these years." Pettigrew laughed. "Flinders, you have become an old softy."

"I think not."

But I think he may be right.

"So now it is birds. What happened to the beautiful women?" Pettigrew shook his head. "Holmes became a beekeeper and now you become a bird watcher. Will it never end?" He closed his newspaper. "I am not sure that I can adjust to this kinder, gentler you."

Flinders held the finch out. "Look again. Did you know that Holmes loved animals too? He rescued stray dogs and regularly contributed to the Royal Humane Society. I met him at one of the meetings."

"Watson doesn't say anything about that."

"Watson leaves out many details."

Pettigrew shook his head. "You have become an aging parent," he said and went back to his reading.

"This from the man who plays 'Twinkle, Twinkle, Little Star' all hours of the day and night." Flinders clattered down the stairs, carefully holding the chick, and yelled over his shoulder, "Mozart must be turning over in his grave by now."

"Mozart is pleased," Pettigrew yelled back.

Flinders reached the tree with the nest and opened his hand. The chick did not move. "I am sorry, my friend," he murmured, gently stroking its head with his forefinger. The chick gave a faint peep, ruffled its feathers, and settled back into his hand. Flinders smiled and then shook his head. "You cannot stay in the hand of a condemned man." He pushed the chick carefully back into the nest. A chorus of excited peeps greeted the fallen one's return. The anxious parents watched the flutter of winglets from the branch above.

Flinders sat down on the iron bench with the Jenny Lind face. He stared at the sphinx a moment and then said, "I have a premonition that some great predator is about to attack." The sightless eyes stared back. "Legend has it that sphinxes devoured humans thousands of years ago." Flinders lit a cigar and blew a smoke ring at the sphinx. "Do you miss gliding through the forest at night in search of human prey?" The morning clouds parted, and a ray of sunshine turned the sphinx's granite head white, but its sightless eyes remained in shadow. "I'll take that as a yes," Flinders said. He laughed and snuffed out the cigar, and opened the back door of his building.

He sensed the finches watching him go.

෬

As far as Flinders knew, Pettigrew never left the flat other than to attend to his work duties. He had fallen in love with a Greek woman long ago. When she died, he'd had no interest in meeting someone else. As he put it, "I have already met the woman in my life. Why should I look further?" Although, sometimes, in the quiet of an evening, he would admit to Flinders that there might have been another woman when he was in the desert.

Flinders had moved out for a while. He had married a woman from Cornwall and fathered a daughter. But both his wife and his baby daughter died in an automobile accident. It was a distant time now, but he remembered returning to the flat a saddened man.

But, as with Pettigrew, there was another, older relationship whose memory floated in the corridors of Flinders's mind.

"You may kiss me on the cheek," she had said. And then she was gone.

And then she was gone. But . . . would she ever be gone?

Once in a while, after a long day at the office, when the sun was setting and the windows of the flat grew dark, Flinders would take a long sip of cognac and speak of her.

Tonight was such a night. They sat in their chairs quietly, sipping wine and reading office materials.

"These case notes are incredibly boring, Thomas."

"Criminals have no imagination, Flinders."

"Thomas," he said, "sometimes, at night, when the flat is still and the street is empty, I can still hear her lullaby. It echoes through my room, just as it echoed through Cleopatra's tomb."

Pettigrew smiled and nodded, closing his eyes. Flinders guessed that his mind had gone back to the time when he, too, was in Egypt. "Egypt," he muttered. That one simple word said everything that could be said.

But as Flinders reflected, it occurred to him that the two of them, professional and hard-bitten detectives that they had become, were haunted by their past. Perhaps that was why they both were determined to control their fate. Both were driven to find something beyond their reach. That was something that bonded them together, that had kept them in the flat all these years.

Cleopatra and Isis watched patiently.

As Flinders recounted, their careers had become impressive. Pettigrew—Doctor Pettigrew, as he was now known in medical circles—was chairman of the board of trustees at a local medical school, a school that had originally been founded by his grandfather a half-century before. As chairman, he emphasized the study of human anatomy, a subject pioneered by both his grandfather and his father. Occasionally, he lectured on anatomical subjects and taught the young doctors to sing "Flow Gently, Sweet Afton." "Flinders," he once said. "My grandfather sang it, my father sang it, and so shall they."

And according to school records, the young doctors developed into a remarkable choir.

On the other hand, Flinders had published several studies of Ptolemaic art and architecture and had become a well-known scholar in his field, much to the delight of his aging uncle and namesake, Sir Flinders Petrie. As a result, Flinders was awarded an honorary chair of classical studies at a local girls' academy. According to legend, on the occasions when he lectured, the students were said to have swooned "en masse."

His nickname among the ladies—much to his amusement—was "the left-handed god." Flinders wrote on blackboards with his left hand and often covered the first row of adoring students with chalk dust. When his lectures were announced, the academy had long waiting lists. There were even rumors of hair-pulling brawls as ladies argued over admission. His entries into the lecture hall were often triumphal marches, and figurative garlands were strewn in his path.

"Good morning, ladies," he would address them.

"Good morning, professor," they would echo back.

Flinders would smile and nod as he strode to and from his lectures, walking through crowds of adoring students. Cheers and enthusiastic screams filled the air. At one such entry, the screams were so loud that a grizzled dean arose from his chair and went to the window of his office to see what the rumpus was about. Flinders could see him looking down on the scene, shaking his head as if to say, "Ah, it's him again."

❧

One morning, as Pettigrew was reading over the mail, he held up a letter addressed to Flinders. "This says that it is from a Miss Barra,"

Pettigrew said, turning the envelope over. "Miss Barra, now who might she be?" He looked up at Flinders, a knowing smile on his face. "I seem to remember her as an American actress with very large eyes. Do you know anything about this?"

Flinders shook his head.

"As I remember, we once had a discussion about you playing a shaykh with a whip. I believe that a certain 'Theda' was to play opposite you. Does that ring a bell?"

"A Miss Barra?" Flinders tried to radiate innocence. "I'm not sure who she is."

"I think she called herself 'the Vamp,'" Pettigrew persisted.

"The Vamp? Would that be short for Vampire?" Flinders stroked his chin. "I don't know any vampires. Except for Heathcliff, of course, and he was a literary figure."

"I'm not asking you about vampires." Pettigrew, apparently, was not to be put off. "I am asking you about an American actress. And you know perfectly well who I am talking about."

"No, I'm still not sure. I do remember a party once. But nothing more."

"A party. What kind of party?"

Flinders shook his head. "Just sort of a vague memory. Party lights and dancing—you know . . . that sort of thing."

"No, I don't know 'that sort of thing.'"

Pettigrew fixed him with a jaundiced eye. "Party lights and dancing, is it?" He rubbed his chin. "Ah, now it comes back to me. You went off to the seaside to visit some 'long lost relatives' from County Cork a couple of months ago. I always wondered about that. Is there something that you would like to tell me now?"

"No, no, it does not come back to me."

"Flinders, really—even the worst criminal could be more convincing than you are."

"All right, I give up."

They both laughed.

But the humdrum continued, and Flinders despaired.

᷎

Their old housekeeper Maggie Burns had retired, returned to Scotland, and eventually died there. Her hand-picked successor, Elise, carried on Maggie's manner of household rule, more gracefully but no less firmly. Elise often smiled and spoke with a faint French accent. Once, Flinders asked her if she was French. "No, my brother and I were raised by my mother," she had answered. "She learned to cook in Paris and spoke perfect French. We copied her accent." She had laughed and shaken her head. Her brown eyes had smiled. She was older than she looked, he had thought. He could see gray streaks in her hair, and there was a tiredness about her despite the smiles. Flinders found her pleasant but stern. "Before she left, Maggie made me promise to serve you mutton," Elise would say as she ladled out the mutton stew.

On a day when he had little else to do, Flinders read his paper and watched her move about the flat. *She is very quick, and she smiles a lot. But I have seen her run to the postbox to deposit a letter before the mail is picked up. When the post arrives, she searches the mail. Sometimes, there is a letter for her. She seizes it and hurries to her room. My instincts tell me that she has children somewhere.*

"Perhaps some beef?" he asked, in regard to that evening's meal. "I understand that beef Wellington is quite delicious."

"Beef Wellington? Now you want beef Wellington?" Elise pondered the thought, an intensity in her thin, drawn face. "You want me to make something out of the Napoleonic Wars?"

"It was a momentary impulse."

Elise was silent for a moment and then smiled. "Maggie said that mutton made you the men that you are. Beef Wellington is not possible. Now please eat your dinners."

I have eaten so much mutton, I may grow horns and climb around steep mountain passes.

Then there was some excitement.

One morning, when all was quiet and the sunlight streamed through the white curtains, Pettigrew rushed into the sitting room, waving a newspaper. "Flinders. The sultan has been overthrown."

"Overthrown?"

"Listen to this. 'Sultan Abdul Hamid the Second has been arrested and taken into captivity. Fighting continues in the Northern provinces. Istanbul has been placed under martial law.'"

"Istanbul is in chaos."

A world vanishes before our eyes.

Pettigrew read further. "'The Imperial harem has been emptied.' See the picture? 'Three thousand women are walking out into the street.'"

Flinders looked. The women did not smile, and some were crying. They carried only coats and luggage. He remembered the harem. What was it that Mariam had said? "They have no place to go. Their carefully guarded world has ended." Then Mariam had looked at him, her eyes sad. "They are like birds in cages—when the cage door is opened, they will be afraid to fly away."

"They look lost," Flinders said. He looked at the sad picture and shook his head. "Their existence is destroyed. There are no more flashing fountains. No more silk and jewels. No more laughter and singing. No more anticipation when they hear the clogs of the sultan."

Kudret said that this world was disappearing. I did not believe him at the time. But he was right. A world of magnificent complexities has been lost forever.

"There is more." Pettigrew spread the paper across his lap. "All of the old empire is crumbling. There are mobs in the streets of major cities."

Kudret's tired eyes had stared across the table at Flinders as he spoke of the old empire. *All of Kudret's carefully orchestrated empire is vanishing. An empire that held the candle of civilization for a thousand years now dissolves into dust.*

How terrible for him.

How terrible for us.

I sense a cataclysm. Lawrence, Bell, and Kudret all knew this was coming. They knew that a war was coming.

Pettigrew scanned the paper. "What will happen to Kudret and Mariam?"

"A good question. Kudret once said, 'I am a kocek. I dance for men; sometimes they want more than dancing. We koceks are like the Empire; we hold society together. When we are gone, remember me and buy a tulip. Its red is my heart.'"

I will buy tulips, my friend. Red tulips for the heart.

"Thomas, he knew." Flinders sighed. "But he could not stop it. How terrible for him."

"We must find out." Pettigrew put the paper down.

"Find out what?" Flinders frowned. "I do not know, but I suspect that the new regime will have little use for koceks and tulips. The Turkish elite will have to find someone other than young boys to entertain them." Flinders shook his head. "Or Assyrian belly dancers." *Her heels rapped on the floor as she moved. She smiled at me and said, "Lift your hip, effendi, and keep moving."*

"I am sure that British Intelligence got them out," Flinders added. "I will cable Lawrence."

He did, but there was no response.

🕉

Weeks passed, and then long months, and then years. The turmoil following Abdul Hamid's overthrow faded from the news. Life returned to normal. The two of them went to work, supervised their staff, and then returned to the flat. Flinders found himself grumbling at every little thing; Pettigrew read his medical journals.

Baker Street remained quiet.

Flinders looked out the windows. Boys played soccer on its cobbles. An occasional cab passed with a rumble of exhaust. Birds chirped and pecked at the curbs. All was mundane bliss, all was mundane boredom.

"Thomas," Flinders said, clearing his throat, "I hear that the city is considering paving over the cobbles."

"Why don't you go over to County Hall and protest? That will give you some excitement."

"I could chain myself to a banister, like those terrible Temperance women."

❧

But nothing happened. Nothing. The big case did not appear. Flinders was in despair. "I wish Uncle Flinders was still around, or maybe even Budge. This sitting around doing nothing is becoming absurd."

"You could try more advertising, you know," Pettigrew suggested. "Or you could go over to the Geographical Society and hob-nob. That used to work. Come to think of it, why don't you write to Sir Leonard and remind him of the time we spent together at Carchemish. He has become even more famous than your late uncle."

After thinking about it, Flinders did write a short note to Sir Leonard Woolley.

But nothing came of it.

❧

Then early one evening, when all hope of adventure seemed to have vanished, Flinders put his penny dreadful down, cocked an ear, and went to the window. "I thought I heard a car stop outside the front door." He lifted the curtain and then turned back to Pettigrew. "Ah ha, I was right. Our prayers may have been answered, and about time too."

"Well?"

"There is a very large black sedan. A person dressed in black robes and a white turban is getting out. He appears to be some sort of important church official, perhaps even an archbishop. He looked over at Holmes's address but turned around and is coming straight here." He trotted about the room, moving chairs and straightening cushions. "Thomas, put those glasses away—we cannot have this place smelling like a tavern when a man of the cloth comes up the stairs. And look sharp—we may have an important visitor."

Flinders tied the sash on his tailored smoking jacket, a Paul Poiret design, very fashionable. *The tailor had said, "You are an elegant man."*

Moments later, Elise rushed upstairs, flustered and out of breath, and announced that "there is some sort of priest waiting below. He looks like the Pope himself." She had barely finished speaking when a small, black-clad man entered the room. Three large, unpleasant-looking men followed him. They looked around the room and scowled.

Pettigrew extended his hand. "To whom have we the pleasure?"

The man smiled; the unpleasant men looked surprised.

The man smiled again and introduced himself: "I am Benyamin bet Shamun. I come as emissary for the Patriarch of the Church of the East. I have come from Baghdad to seek your help. These men are my bodyguards. My good friend Sir Leonard Woolley has recommended you. He said that you recovered a missing statue of Aphrodite against all odds, and that you may be able to assist us."

Flinders bowed. "We are honored, your grace. Please do sit down. How may we help you?"

The emissary sat down on the art deco couch. He nervously fingered his golden cross and rearranged himself several times. His men placed themselves behind the couch and folded their arms. Flinders noticed a small twitch. *The man is very concerned about something,* he thought. The bodyguards frowned.

"I have come as a last resort. A small casket containing the relics of the Apostle Thomas has been taken and must be found."

"The Apostle Thomas?" Flinders shifted in his chair.

"Yes." The emissary took out a rosary and thumbed it. "Let me explain. In the first century after Christ's death, his disciples fanned out and created new churches. Peter went north to Rome; Thomas went east. He planted the Church of the East in Mesopotamia, and it spread rapidly through Persia, India, and even as far as China and Japan."

"I know something of the travels of the Apostles." Flinders rubbed a kneecap and recrossed his legs. "I was a classical scholar before I became a detective."

The emissary sighed. "Christianity and the Church of the East flourished in the Middle East until the seventh century. Then Omar and the Muslims conquered the area." He buried his face in his hands. "Now we are reduced to enclaves in Muslim territories."

"How terrible."

"Yes, our crosses are hidden, our bells are silent, and our worshippers live in fear."

"But you continue to worship."

"Yes, we survived and continued to worship."

"I see."

"We have always cherished our founder's relics. In the thirteenth century, the Apostle's bones were returned from India, where he died, to a basilica in Italy. Then they were transferred to the Church of the East in Erbil. We cared for them for centuries, but now, they have been stolen."

"How so?" Pettigrew asked. "Please tell us the particulars."

"Where can I start? It is too awful." The emissary rocked back and forth on the sofa. Its frame squeaked as he moved. "The Apostle's bones were contained in a silver casket. The Pope himself commissioned the design; we were honored. We displayed it in the basilica. Thousands of the faithful passed by it every day."

The emissary sat up and adjusted the gold cross that hung on his neck.

"Day and night it was guarded by four strong men. They were descendants of warriors. The blood of Assyria was in their veins. No one could pass by them." He paused for breath. "Then one morning, we found the casket missing; the guards were dead, their throats slit. They were lying in pools of their own blood."

He fingered the beads. "The Holy Scriptures were desecrated; the altar was on its side."

"Their throats were slit?" Pettigrew cocked his head to one side.

The emissary nodded. "The blood of Assyria was everywhere."

The three men scowled.

"They desecrated the church." The emissary's eyes were pools of horror. "They entered a sacred place and ravaged it."

"A sacred place," Flinders murmured. He leaned back in his chair and stared at the carpet. The scene of the crime filled his mind. *Horrified priests stare at the scene. Four bodies lie on the basilica floor; blood stains it. The altar is overturned; candles are scattered on the marble tiles. Gilded fragments gape where a holy relic once rested. Nuns lament in anguish.*

"How could men do that?" The emissary's voice cracked.

"Unfortunately," Flinders said quietly, "there are men who do such things."

Pettigrew nodded. "That is why we became detectives long ago."

Long ago, we made the decision to become detectives. We committed ourselves to hunt down those who would destroy humanity. But the cost has been as terrible to us as it was to Holmes.

Flinders looked at Pettigrew. His face was drawn and pale. Tunnels of light from the setting sun swept slowly across the seated figures. Their faces changed in the shifting light. Traffic rumbled from somewhere in the street below.

"So, tell us more, please," Flinders finally said.

I think we are about to meet an old adversary.

"We removed the bodies and cleaned up the blood." The emissary shivered. "We swore the priests and the nuns to a vow of silence. Then we announced that the bones were temporarily removed to repair the casket. No one knows that they have been stolen."

"Was there anything else?" Pettigrew leaned forward in his seat.

"Yes." The emissary reached into a leather purse and pulled out a crumpled piece of paper. Its gold lettering gleamed in the lamplight. "We found this."

"Let me see that." Flinders stood. He reached out and took the paper. He frowned and looked at Pettigrew, who remained in his chair. "I have seen something like this before. Yes, yes, this is an Ottoman firman. Your thief and murderer was a hashshashin. Your guards stood no chance against him. You are lucky that no one else was killed." He looked at Pettigrew. "Thomas, I think that we are about to meet the Veiled One again."

Pettigrew nodded. "It appears so."

Flinders handed the paper to Pettigrew. "This is a death sentence."

"We have seen that before."

"There is more." The emissary leaned back against the cushions. "These are dangerous times. My people are attacked daily. Villages are raided, men and boys are killed, and young women are carried off." He put his face in his hands. "The Patriarch has taken refuge in the mountains." The men standing behind the couch glared.

"Your villages were attacked?" Flinders frowned. "Please tell me more."

"We call this the 'Year of the Sayfo.'"

"The Sayfo?"

"Yes, 'Sayfo' means 'sword' in our language. Our people are being put to the sword."

The emissary bowed his head.

Flinders looked at Pettigrew. "Thomas," he said, "this is no ordinary case."

Pettigrew nodded but was quiet.

"What you ask us to do is very difficult," Flinders said. He paced in front of the window. "There are no witnesses. There is no crime scene. We have nothing to go on." He went to the mantel and lounged against it. Cleopatra looked down over his head. "You must understand that the task is almost impossible."

He looked up at the portrait.

You command me to do this.

The emissary slumped. "What can we do?"

Flinders sighed. "We know who did this. We barely escaped with our lives the last time we met him." Flinders stood up and went to the window and pulled the white curtains wide. He looked out. *What is it that I look for?*

"Thomas, are you willing to cross swords with the Veiled One again?"

Pettigrew rubbed his shoulder. "It still hurts when the weather is cold." Then he smiled. "But perhaps it could use some exercise."

"It will mean going back."

"Perhaps I may find someone."

"You may not like what you find."

And I may not like what I find either.

"Thomas, you once looked out this window and said, 'The far pavilions it is.' Now it is my turn to say it." Flinders closed the curtains and turned to the emissary. "The far pavilions it is. We will take your case and recover the Apostle's bones," he said. "We will need a retainer and an expense account."

The emissary took a large checkbook out from under his robes and wrote out a draft. Pettigrew examined it, smiled, and said, "The Bank of England—very nice." He put it in a large notebook.

The emissary smiled. "You were expecting drachmas?"

"The thought had occurred to me."

"King Herod is long dead and so is his currency," the emissary laughed. "Our religion may be ancient, but our banking is quite up to date."

The emissary stood up; the men scowled. Flinders bowed, and they left. As the door closed behind them, Pettigrew frowned. "Cleopatra was not enough, now you want to find the bones of the Apostle Thomas? Flinders, you are always building fairy castles in the air."

We now cross the Rubicon. The Rubicon. How fitting—we return to an ancient world, and that ancient world returns to the present.

Pettigrew's voice was quiet. "You tempt me, sir."

"Whatever happened to the young student who looked at the ants?"

"He grew old."

"Are you so sure about that?"

"Fairy castles, is it?'

Flinders laughed. "Fairy castles are the best kind of castles. Yes, I think that finding an Apostle's bones would be just the right thing for us."

"Once, we found Cleopatra. Was that not enough?"

"No, it is never enough. We must recover the Apostle's bones."

"You drag me into impossible cases."

"And we succeed against all odds."

"We do succeed, somehow."

"As I said, finding the Apostle's bones is just our ticket."

"But of course, it is." Pettigrew grinned. "Now, my detecting friend, how do you propose to find out where these bones have gone?" Pettigrew sat down and put his head in his hands. "Flinders, you look out the windows every day, searching for what, I do not know. You drink like a fish. You imagine impossible tigers. And now you have gotten us into an impossible quest."

"A quest is always impossible." Flinders smirked. "If it were possible, everyone would do it."

"You are a modern-day Don Quixote."

"And so are you."

"Indeed, you may be right."

Pettigrew stood up. "Flinders, we have taken the man's money. And he wasn't just a man—he was the Patriarch's emissary."

"Let me have a look at the check." Flinders looked up. "It has a patriarchal seal." His eyes widened. "Thomas, I don't think he was an emissary."

"What do you mean?"

"Thomas, I think we just had a visit from the Patriarch himself." Flinders shook his head. "And I thought he was an archbishop."

"He must have been extraordinarily concerned to make such a dangerous trip. Even in disguise."

"He said that his people were being put to the sword."

"The 'Sayfo,' he called it." Pettigrew frowned. "'The Sword'—the word says it all, a description of mass killing."

"Reason enough for a Patriarch to travel."

"Indeed so."

"And then we promised him that we would recover his relic."

Pettigrew nodded. "Indeed we did."

"Then we must do as we promised."

"Indeed, we shall. It is a matter of honor." Pettigrew frowned. "As it was, once before."

"We must enter the world of a massacre," Flinders said. But he wondered what they would find. He was not optimistic. *The world of a massacre—would that I should never have to experience such a world.*

Pettigrew rubbed his forehead. "So, how do you propose to do this?"

"I know a priest."

"You know a priest." Pettigrew shook his head in disbelief. "Well, that is indeed wonderful."

"No, no, you don't understand." Flinders held a hand up. "He works for British Intelligence. He is most knowledgeable."

"And you think that British Intelligence knows where Saint Thomas's bones lie hidden?"

"It is a start."

"But not much of one."

"You may be surprised."

"These Intelligence people are like fleas. They are all over the place. Did not you have enough of them in Istanbul?" Pettigrew frowned. "I remember Kudret and his dancing koceks. You made me dress as a kocek."

"And you were wonderful," Flinders said. "You looked marvelous in your red vest and gold earrings." He chuckled. "You were very natural . . . very natural, indeed."

Pettigrew glowered.

Flinders danced around the sitting room. "Mariam said that when you danced, you floated like foam on the waves."

"Never mind that," Pettigrew growled. "So, you have found an Intelligence agent disguised as a priest. I suppose that now you will want me to wear a cassock and a turned-around collar. Bedouin robes were not enough?"

"You once looked like a bedouin shaykh, and now you can look like a young pope."

"A young pope, is it?"

"With that face of yours, you could pass for a Borgia." Flinders draped on an imaginary cassock and surplice and postured. "It is a wonderful disguise. Remember Father Brown, the young man who wrote to me? No one ever looked at him twice."

"Yes, but he was in England. The Ottoman Empire, or what is left of it, is an entirely different place."

"Nonsense. You'll be fine." Flinders thought a moment. "I knew we should have taken up acting. You would have made a wonderful Hamlet, wandering around the stage in a muddle." Then he grinned. "Actually, you wouldn't have to act the muddle part, you could just be yourself."

Pettigrew laughed. "I think you are the actor here."

Flinders postured. "I have considered becoming a thespian."

"And I suppose you would play opposite Sarah Bernhardt?"

"Indeed so, like that fellow Maurice Barrymore." He strutted. "'To be, or not to be. That is the question.'" He smiled. "You must admit that was good."

"Never mind." Pettigrew scowled. "So where is this pesky priest?"

"At the Ashmolean Library." Flinders grinned. "Surely you remember it from your school days."

Pettigrew laughed. "As I said many years ago, there is no stopping you. A priest it is."

"Pack, Thomas. We search for an Apostle. The game is afoot."

Pettigrew frowned. "We are like old warhorses. The bugle has sounded."

"Not too old, I hope. Thomas, should I bring my pistols?"

"Not unless you are you planning to shoot someone at Oxford."

⌘

They took the train to Oxford. Elise packed them mutton sandwiches. "Are you sure that you are bundled up? Maggie made me promise to see that you don't catch cold."

And to Flinders it did seem like old times.

At least for the moment.

And for a moment, it did seem to him that the game might truly be afoot.

They took the train to Oxford the next day. The train rumbled along, and then slowed. Trees crawled by. Flinders looked out the coach window at the passing woods and, for one brief moment, he thought he saw a tiger staring at him. Its sinister form was bright against the dark tree line. He blinked. *My eyes are playing tricks on me*. The train sped up. He looked again; the scene was dark except for the flashes of light from the coach windows reflected from the passing roadway.

Pettigrew dozed off in the seat facing him. The newspaper he was reading had fallen to the floor. The compartment reeked of stale cigar smoke and stale newspapers. Flinders could see conductors walking up and down the outside corridor. He rubbed a hand across his face and leaned back in the seat. Lights flashed by the compartment window. *My Irish imagination has taken control of me. First, I saw serpents in Egypt, now I see tigers in Oxfordshire. I've been reading too many dreadfuls.*

My Irish mother once said, "You've got the gift, so you do." But what kind of gift allows me to see the past but not the future?

His eyes closed. "But maybe the past is the future." The rocking of the train lulled him. *The Roman world swims in my mind. Christians walk in chains before my eyes. A tiger lurks in the colosseum of my mind.* He dozed and then slept. Signal lights glowed and disappeared; crossings glittered and clanged past.

The tiger waited in the forest of his mind.

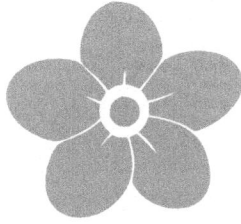

TWO

Ad Limina Apostolorum

"Do you miss your frogs, Thomas?" Flinders teased as they walked across the manicured path. "I remember that your room was littered with jars of strange specimens and frog parts. The smell was terrific."

"Not as bad as that from your mummy wrappings," Pettigrew noted, lifting a finger to his nose. "I can still smell the stench."

"Not true at all." Flinders grinned. "Most wrappings smell dusty, and there was only one that had an odor." He smiled. "It somehow got wet in transit. So I brought it home from class."

"That was an unbelievably bad idea. We had to evacuate the dorm. The deans were furious."

"No one is perfect."

Bright streams of sunlight bounced off the Ashmolean's Doric columns. Birds chirped and the air was warm. "It's good to be back," Flinders said as they climbed the broad steps and passed under the

Greek revival lintel. "You know, Thomas, it's been years, but nothing has changed." Students milled happily through the bronze doors. They laughed and burbled. "It is as though we have gone back in time." A marble entry opened before Flinders. "Look at those tiles—I remember the scratches on them." Flinders spread his arms. "I am a young student again—I am carefree."

"You put some of those scratches on them yourself," Pettigrew said. "As I remember, it was very late at night. The staff had left, and the library was dark."

"Not totally dark—there were a few night-lights."

"You pried the back door open with your saber."

"The lock was rusty."

"You rushed in and started waving your saber."

"I had just come from team practice." Flinders demonstrated a lunge. "I was the captain."

"You said that you were looking for a book."

"Yes, it was an original copy of *Cyrano de Bergerac*. They wouldn't let me check it out—they said that I had to read it in the reading room. Stuffy devils."

"You think that everyone who disagrees with you is a stuffy devil."

"Well, they most certainly are."

"We got inside, and you found the book," Pettigrew said. "Then you opened a large flask filled with cognac."

"The night was cold." Flinders remembered it well. There was a particular chill in the air that night.

"You pulled the cork and yelled, 'Here's to Cyrano.'"

"Cognac is good for the soul." And it had been good for eliminating the chill in the air.

"We drank the cognac, and you made me read passages while you demonstrated your skill with the saber." Pettigrew put a finger to his nose. "Something about a nose, I think."

Flinders struck a pose. "Yes, the nose, 'tis a rock, a peak, a cape, a peninsula!'" He flourished an imaginary hat. "Cyrano had such elegant lines."

"Ah, I remember that flourish."

"'A great nose may be an index of a great soul.'"

"Very good."

Pettigrew pushed Flinders toward a reception desk. "But after a couple of swigs of cognac your blade kept hitting the marble tiles. The noise was terrific. It was as though Siegfried was pounding on a dragon." Pettigrew chuckled. "And sometimes you missed the dragon."

"No one is perfect," Flinders scoffed. "And, besides, dragons are hard to hit. They are very fast, you know."

"At least you didn't start singing, 'yo, ho, ho.'"

"We *were* in a library."

"Yo, ho, ho." Pettigrew's deep bass rumbled through the library.

Students looked up from their books. Librarians huffed and lowered their reading glasses.

"You really are a troll." Flinders covered a sly smile with his hand. "And you are becoming more trollish as you age."

"A troll, sir?" Pettigrew said, lifting an eyebrow and crossing his arms.

"Yes, perhaps from a long line of trolls. Someone should really research your genealogy."

"Yo, ho, ho," Pettigrew sang again. "Fee, fie, foh, fum, I smell the blood of an Englishman!"

Students clapped; librarians scowled.

"I say it again: you are a troll." Flinders could not contain the laugh. "And worse yet, you have mixed up the lyrics."

"I should have brought my trumpet."

"You don't have a trumpet, and now you're making a spectacle of yourself."

"Details, as you would say."

An elderly librarian appeared at Pettigrew's elbow. "Could you gentlemen please be quiet?" His mutton chops quivered with annoyance.

Pettigrew peered down at him.

"Dear me." Flinders looked askance. "I am shocked—simply *shocked*—at this behavior. First the trumpet, then the piano, and now a crazed character from a Wagnerian opera."

"I was feeling the zephyrs of my youth."

"Zephyrs of your youth?"

"Indeed, I have become a schoolboy again." Pettigrew looked owl-ish. "I believe you said something similar."

"You mean you have regressed to childhood."

"Once a man, twice a child."

"Oh, for heaven's sake."

"Anyway." Pettigrew laughed. "Your racket brought the caretaker in on the run, and we had to climb out a window to escape."

"It seemed like a good idea at the time."

"But you got tangled up with your saber and fell in the mud."

"Even Cyrano had off days."

Then Pettigrew frowned. "But that was long ago. We have changed. We are no longer carefree."

"Perhaps you are right." Flinders felt the smile fade from his face. "But all the same . . ." He strode forward. "Let us find this priest. He said to meet him at the entrance to the collections." He approached the desk and handed the student behind it his old student card. "We would like to go into the stacks."

The student looked at the card and then at Flinders. She turned the card over. "I've never seen one this old. We don't use these anymore." She looked up. "My father had one." She stood up and turned to go. "I shall have to ask."

Flinders frowned.

Pettigrew smiled. "It could have been worse. She could have said 'my grandfather.' There is hope for you yet."

Flinders watched the student disappear. Then she came back. "I'm sorry . . ."

"Don't bother—I'll vouch for them." A tall, portly man in a black suit with a white collar stepped out of nowhere. "Flinders, it's good to see you. I got your cable. And Doctor Pettigrew . . . how nice." He smiled. "My real name is Macgregor, but my code name is Father Divinius. But just call me Divinius." He opened an iron door behind the desk. "Follow me."

"Divinius?" Pettigrew asked. "Do you speak Latin?"

"No, but we try to be academic."

He led them through the door and to a circular iron stairway. They descended. Their boots clanged on the stair treads. Floors of shelves flowed by, the rows stretching into infinity in the darkness—rows of books marching away. Down, down, down. *I have been here before,* thought Flinders. *I am going into the underworld again.* A gray shape fluttered past. "Was that a bird?"

"Yes, there are many starlings that nest in the stacks. They've nested here for ages."

"It comes back to me now. I remember the droppings."

Flinders's hands slid down the iron railings. Their ridges brushed his fingers, and their touch brought back memories. The sound of their footsteps on the stairs rang in his ears. His arms felt the weight of books—an old world opened in his imagination, and a past suddenly came alive. *Strange how the touch of a railing opens a lost window. The hall was long. He was late to class. He rounded a corner and skidded to a stop. A figure kneeled before him—a young man looking intently at a stream of ants climbing the wall. A blonde head looked up. "My name is Thomas."*

Flinders sniffed. "I smell cooking."

Divinius looked over his shoulder. "Of course. Families have been living here for decades. Many of them work in the Museum. Most of them live among the Sumerian exhibits." He laughed. "Some of them are quite odd. There is one old scholar who came in a few years ago, right after his friend, General Gordon, was killed at Khartoum. I think the trauma of the general's death addled the old man's mind. We know he's still alive because he sends the other librarians notes regularly. My guess is that he is somewhere in the Nabatean collection. We call him the 'Phantom of the Library' . . . after the French novel."

A face flashed in front of Flinders's eyes. *I think I met him once. He had wild eyes and carried an armload of tattered books. When he saw me, he turned and disappeared into thin air. A tattered old paper curled to the ground where he once stood. I wasn't sure that he was real.*

They stepped off the stairs and into the gloom. Divinius pushed them toward a small door with a dirty pane. The sign on it read SUPPLY CLOSET. "Come in, come in," he said, unlocking the door with a large key and pushing the door open. "We located our Intelligence headquarters here because nobody ever comes down. We thought about an abandoned railway station, but this is cozier and much more refined." The door opened to reveal a large room packed with desks, tables, and shelves. A Marconi stood in one corner and made mechanical noises. "Observe." Divinius pointed to it. "We have the latest in modern technology." He bent over it for a moment. "We receive many cables—I am in contact with the entire world here." He patted his large stomach. "I keep the pulse of the planet, don't you know." He gestured at some chairs. "Do sit down. Just push those folders off. You can set them on the floor."

"Where is everybody?" Flinders glanced around the empty office.

"They're on vacation." Divinius smiled. "There was a lull in events, so I gave them the week off." He sat at the far end of a table. "A happy Intelligence is a good Intelligence."

"Of course."

"And besides, we have civil service holidays."

Flinders looked at the wall. "Isn't that a portrait of Mycroft Holmes?"

A huge oil painting of Mycroft smiled down from an ornate gilt frame.

"Indeed, it is. Mycroft was the founder of this operation." Divinius puffed with pride. "I was personally trained by him. We used to sit for hours in the Diogenes Club and pass notes." Divinius rubbed his stomach; his gold watch and chain rattled. "He was a great man. He used to say, 'A firm stomach leads to a firm brain.' He coordinated all Intelligence activity for years. Now I do it." He leaned forward. "I fancy that I even look like him."

Flinders looked at Pettigrew, who smiled faintly.

"But you didn't come here to listen to tales." Divinius lit a cigarette. "You want to know about Saint Thomas the Apostle."

"Yes, his bones have been stolen and we are commissioned to find and return them. We believe the Veiled One is responsible."

"The Veiled One." Divinius scowled. "A very bad character. We have heard of him many times."

"So we have come to you." Flinders held out the firman.

Divinius took a large magnifying glass from a shelf and examined the vellum. "I have seen these before." He sighed. "Once, when I was very young and new in the Civil Service, I was asked to investigate the murder of an agent." He frowned. "Another agent and I went to the address where the murder occurred. We opened the door. The room was empty except for a table. A severed head was on it. The smell was awful. Flies buzzed about the head, and its eyes were sewn shut."

He held up the vellum. "A vellum like this was in the head's mouth. Ever since, I have hated flies."

Flinders looked at Pettigrew. "Your father said something like this. Something about a man sewn up inside a mummy."

Divinius covered his face with his hands. "I've never seen anything like that." He shook his head. "And I hope that I never see that again." He looked up at Flinders. His face was suddenly old and tired. "Never again."

"I am so sorry," Flinders said softly. "We have witnessed similar killings."

"Thank you." Divinius managed a wan smile.

"But you want to know about Saint Thomas." His face brightened, and he patted the table with both hands. "Well, then you have arrived at the right place." He waved at the cabinet, which lined the walls. "We keep track of everything ecumenical, and I must say that some of the greatest theologians of our time have worked for us." Divinius smiled. "One of our agents regularly sermonized here at Christ Church. I don't suppose that either of you attend church?"

Flinders did not respond, and neither did Pettigrew.

He shrugged his shoulders and muttered, "No? Too bad, too bad. What is the world coming to?"

"Do go on," Pettigrew insisted.

"First, let me show you around." Divinius smiled broadly, as if forgiving them for their sins. "We have the finest collection of religious items in the world." He pushed them through a small door, into a small room lined with glass cases. "Look at these," he said, pointing to a case filled with chalices. "These are the goblets the popes used to drink from. See that small one on the end?" He opened the glass door. "That is from the time of Christ. We had a request to find the Holy Grail, but this was the best we could do."

"Amazing," Flinders said, reaching out to touch the goblet.

"And over here is a selection of papal and other religious robes." Divinius suddenly looked serious. He frowned. "We also had a request to find the robe that Jesus wore on the cross. But some Roman ran off with it." Divinius clucked and shook his head.

Pettigrew nodded. "I remember reading something about that."

"His name was Marcellus," Flinders interjected. "You forget I studied the Classics." *But what really happened then? My mind sees the image of a Roman soldier holding out a tattered cloth robe. His face is filled with reverence.*

"And here," Divinius beamed, "is our collection of papal headdresses. Our collection easily matches that in the Vatican Museums. Would you like to try one on?"

"No, but I think Thomas would." Flinders grinned. "It would go perfectly with his wig."

Pettigrew scowled, shaking his head.

Flinders examined a headdress. "Why do you have so many collections?" he asked.

"We are a museum, you know. It is quite appropriate."

"Very logical."

"But here—" Divinius waved them to a low table covered with glasses of various shapes. "Here is our collection of glasses the Borgias used to fill with poison." He smiled. "Without doubt, it is the finest in the world. Doris is our official poison curator. She has managed to match most of them with the correct poison." He beamed. "No mean feat, I assure you—the Borgias were very clever in concealing their poisons." He chuckled. "And occasionally, Doris makes the real thing. We once had to evacuate the building because of the poisonous vapors. The acid from them ate the nose of a bust of Puzur-Asher. The museum curators were furious."

"Very interesting." Flinders smiled. "And I suppose you have poison parties."

"How clever of you to guess." Divinius laughed. "Every year we have a 'Borgia Ball.' We all dress up as Borgias—I dress as Pope Callixtus III. And I must say that I am magnificent. I have received many compliments. Doris fills all the glasses with colored brandy, made by local monks of course, and we roister the night away."

"The thought boggles my mind," Pettigrew muttered under his breath. "Dancing popes. . . . What is this place that Flinders has gotten me into?"

He frowned at Flinders, and Flinders smiled innocently back.

Divinius looked at Flinders knowingly. "Once in a while, famous prime ministers join in the revelry." He pointed to a photograph pinned on the wall. "Prime Minister Asquith himself came last year. He was dressed as Innocent the Third. His costume was splendid."

"I can imagine," Flinders said. "But, about Saint Thomas."

"Saint Thomas, an interesting man," said Father Divinius.

"How so?"

"I know all about him."

"And?"

"I shall show you."

Divinius pulled out a drawer. Parchment manuscripts fell on the floor. A small mouse looked out and then disappeared.

"You are in luck." Divinius smiled broadly. "I am also the prefect of the Religious Studies unit. But most of the reporting on Eastern churches is done by Father Boris out of our Silk Road office in Balkh. He has a wonderful collection of icons. You should really see it." Divinius thought a moment. "Balkh is a hard assignment. Father Boris is lonely. He sometimes amuses himself by singing in the Balkh Opera."

"He sings?"

"Yes, he is quite fond of Russian operas, especially when he gets to play the tzar. He has a magnificent bass." Divinius flicked an ash off his sleeve. "We send him cases of brandy, made by monks of course. A professional courtesy, you might say."

Flinders chuckled. "He must smile a lot."

"Come to think of it, some of his reports are little disorganized." Divinius looked thoughtful. "In fact, one of them was written on the back of an icon. We have no idea how it got there." He rolled his eyes. "It was a twelfth-century icon depicting Saint George—England's patron saint. We thought at first that there must be a hidden message. But no, there was nothing, just some brown stains." Divinius shook his head.

"Saint Thomas," Pettigrew said. "We are here about Saint Thomas."

"All right. Let's see what he has sent us on Saint Thomas." Divinius rummaged around in a corner. "Ah yes, here they are, the reports of the reliquary subcommittee. Reliquaries are an especially important concern. We have quite a large collection of reliquaries. It's in that little room over there." Divinius pointed. "Reliquaries and the remains they contain are an especially important concern. Our prize possession is Robert the Bruce's heart."

"Robert the Bruce's heart?"

"I'm almost afraid to ask," Flinders said. "How did you manage that?"

"Well . . ." Divinius fingered his lapels. "The casket containing it was thrown at the Moors by Sir Douglas, in the thirteen hundreds. It was recovered from the battlefield and buried at Melrose Abbey. Later, it was disinterred, and we bought it at auction." Divinius puffed out his chest. "I myself cast the winning bid."

"I never would have guessed," Pettigrew stated flatly.

Divinius smiled.

"Was it expensive?" Flinders asked.

"Not really. Antiques don't bring much anymore."

Flinders nodded. "How true. No one cares about the past nowadays." *Except me.*

"Do you have many antique hearts in your collection?"

"No, only this one." Divinius sighed. "I bid on Richard the First's heart, but some French churchmen outbid me."

"Is the heart in a reliquary?"

"No, it's not controversial."

"Controversial?"

"Relics are difficult to deal with." Divinius looked stern. "You never know when they are going to pop up and start some religious uprising."

"Relics start uprisings?"

Divinius shook his head. "Fortunately, not that often. There was a problem with the missing right hand of Saint Stephen a few years ago. It was stolen and then recovered under mysterious circumstances. Anyway, a riot broke out and downtown Budapest was set on fire."

"And the hand?"

"It was returned to its proper place, in accordance with church rules."

"Church rules?"

"Churches have rules about relics and their reliquaries. Remember, relics are the physical remains of saints—you can't just have them lying about."

"But, about Saint Thomas." Pettigrew scowled again at Flinders.

"Very logical." Flinders counted his fingers. "You can't just leave them lying about."

"Never mind that."

Divinius opened a large leather folder. "Let me go down the list of saints. Ah, I have it, just after Saint Theophanes the Confessor." He pulled out a large file and read: "Saint Thomas, sometimes called 'doubting Thomas,' was one of the more ardent disciples." Divinius put on a large pair of tinted green glasses and leafed through more pages. "Peter founded the Church of Rome, and Andrew founded the Church of Constantinople." Divinius leafed through more pages. "Thomas went to India and founded the Church of the East. The Church of the East and its offshoots dominated the Middle East for centuries." He took a deep breath and looked owlishly over the green lenses. "It was a grand time for Christianity."

"Please get to the point." Pettigrew fidgeted in his chair and stared at the file.

Flinders rested his chin on his hands in thought. *But what is the point?* he wondered. *The Apostles walked with dust on their feet to spread their word. They sweated in the sun and the heat. Roman soldiers laughed at them and prodded them with lances. Some were crucified and felt agony as nails were driven into their hands. And then they suffered slow suffocation on crosses. What manner of men were these, to suffer so much for their convictions?*

Divinius continued to read from the folder. "Thomas died in India. He is one of the original saints of Christianity. His bones are venerated. Christians make pilgrimages to visit them." He paused, resting a finger on a specific place in the text. "It says here that his remains are worshipped like those of Bernadette at Lourdes. My, that is impressive." Divinius pulled the glasses down his nose. "You have got your work cut out for you. The reliquary of Saint Thomas is quite small and easily transported."

Flinders remembered the emissary's drawn face. *The Patriarch wants us to recover the bones of an Apostle. The Apostle's followers were people that marched, singing, into the Colosseum and certain death. People who walked onto the bloody sands and laughed at animals' fangs. No wonder the might of Rome could not withstand them. The Patriarch asks us to return to the first century and enter the world of Rome and bring back the Apostle's bones.*

"What would be the result of the theft?" Flinders asked.

Divinius frowned. "If the Veiled One can carry off Saint Thomas's bones and display them as relics of a false religion, he could possibly destroy the remaining Christian Churches in the Middle East."

It seemed impossible to Flinders that this could be the case. "Would no one oppose this?"

Divinius shook his head. "There would be little that anyone could do against his propaganda. There would be mobs in the streets."

"Mobs in the streets?"

"As you know, the sultan has been overthrown. The old Ottoman government is divided into factions. I have a report somewhere by our Ottoman expert." Divinius shuffled some files. "Yes, here it is. It is quite complete."

"You have an Ottoman expert?"

"Father Christmas." Divinius smiled. "He is most well-informed."

"Father Christmas is your expert on the Ottoman empire?" Flinders shook his head—Divinius had to be pulling their legs.

"That's a code name—his real name is George." Divinius tapped the table with his glasses. "Or Giorgios, as he calls himself. He runs the dragoman squadron. His men have access to everybody of importance."

"The dragon squadron?" Pettigrew looked skeptical.

"No, the *dragoman* squadron."

"So is a dragoman the son of a dragon?" Flinders asked.

"My gracious." Divinius clucked in disbelief. "Dragons do not have sons. You miss the point."

"Please enlighten us."

"Dragomen are the official translators between the Ottoman elite and Arab, Persian, and other communities," Divinius explained. "They speak many languages, and they know everything. We've been recruiting them for years." Divinius looked up at the Mycroft portrait. "*He* would be proud. They call themselves 'the Gray Ears.'"

"The Gray Ears?"

"They are all elderly."

"Of course they are." Pettigrew rolled his eyes.

"Moving on . . ." Divinius frowned. "We still do not know what the new rulers will do." Divinius waved the file. "There are increasing attacks on Christian communities by Cossack irregulars. Armenian shops have been ransacked—their owners have been beaten. Assyrian villages have been burned."

"Indeed." Flinders nodded. "That is why the Patriarch's emissary was so upset."

"Yes." Divinius put the file down and stared into space. "It would make the Mahdi's uprising in the Sudan look like one of Baden-Powell's campouts." He frowned again. "This is a very dangerous time. I wish Mycroft were here to give us guidance."

Mycroft beamed down from his wall.

The Marconi clacked a few times and then snapped to a stop. Papers rustled on the shelves. Muffled steps disappeared on the iron stairs outside. Divinius lit another cigarette and blew a smoke ring. The smoke circled in a halo around his head.

"Yes, our work is cut out for us," Flinders murmured.

Pettigrew looked at Flinders. "Your little adventure may be much more serious than you thought."

More serious indeed. The gates open, the white sands shine, the crowd roars, and the Christians look at me as they walk to their death.

Divinius continued. "You want to know about this Veiled One fellow. Not a nice man. We've been on to him for years." He rummaged in one of the shelves and produced a thick folder. "Let me see what we have here." Divinius opened the folder and flipped through its pages. "Ah, yes . . . here is the latest report written by one of our agents. It says that the Veiled One is expanding his power throughout the region." He turned some pages. "The list of people he has murdered is impressive." He thumbed a few stained photographs. "These are pictures of villages that he destroyed. Do you want to see them?"

Pettigrew took the pictures, grimaced, and then handed them to Flinders.

I already know about that. The shaykh described it, long ago. "Black birds feeding," he had said.

"He may have had a hand in the sultan's overthrow." He looked up. "Ah, here is a photograph of him. It's slightly out of focus, but it's the best we could get." Divinius handed it to Flinders.

Flinders saw the blurred figure of a man standing in a street. It was taken through a window high above. The man wore a silver veil that covered his nose and mouth. He had on a black suit and was pointing at something. He had an aura of menace that came through even in the photograph. In front of him were kneeling men. Men with swords stood behind them. *He is ordering an execution.* Flinders passed the photograph to Pettigrew.

Pettigrew nodded soberly. "Chilling."

"Yes, the report says that it took several blows to sever their heads," Divinius added. "The photographer reported that the Veiled One laughed all the while and then kicked at the heads as they rolled in the dust."

"He looks bulky in that suit."

"We think he wears some kind of armor under the jacket. Perhaps a chain mail shirt."

"I see," Pettigrew said. He handed the photograph back. "Is there more?"

"The report stops here, mid-sentence. The agent didn't finish it." Divinius took off his glasses. "We found it in his office. We think that he was going to add more details from further investigation, but he had a terrible accident and died."

"Curious. Are you sure it was an accident?" Flinders leaned forward in his chair.

Divinius rolled his eyes. "Come to think of it, the accident happened in Baghdad."

"What kind of accident?"

"An automobile accident. His car was destroyed by a large lorry."

"A lorry?"

"It came out of nowhere and then disappeared."

Divinius lit another cigarette. "The circumstances were unclear. It could have just been an accident, but let me think; there may be more. Mycroft once said that truth is never pure or simple." He took a breath. "We think he was on the way back to the office to finish the report." Divinius sighed. "We have lost other agents in Baghdad under mysterious circumstances."

Flinders nodded. "You are dealing with the Veiled One. He does not play games."

Divinius put the folder on the table.

Smoke drifted upward, and the room was silent.

Flinders stood up. "You must excuse me. It's been a long train ride."

"The loo is over there," Divinius pointed. "Across from the Middle Dynasty collection. Mind you don't trip on the Akkadian tablets." Divinius laughed. "And be sure to duck your head as you go in. The Sword of Damocles hangs over the door. Sometimes people get stabbed."

"The Sword of Damocles over a loo, but of course."

Flinders found the loo and returned through the stacks. He had almost reached the supply closet when a figure emerged from the rows of books; the figure grabbed him and planted a wet kiss firmly on his cheek. Flinders disentangled himself and pushed the figure away. He saw a small woman with a large head of hair and enormous rimmed glasses. The woman giggled and disappeared in a cloud of paper dust.

Flinders dusted himself off and peered into the rows of books. An Assyrian fertility figurine in the form of a parrot peered back from the end of a row. Her large eyes and parrot face smiled at him. *Well, at least you didn't kiss me.* Then he laughed. *I wonder how it would feel to be kissed by a three-thousand-year-old parrot.*

Flinders made his way back to the office. "A woman kissed me," he told Pettigrew and Divinius, gesturing toward the dark corridors of books. "Who was that woman? For a moment, I thought I was in the middle of *Jane Eyre*. Bertha Mason just flew at me." He frowned, shaking his head. "I have never liked Brontë's writings, and now I know why. 'There was no possibility of taking a walk that day,' and there was no possibility of a trip to the loo today."

"Very good." Divinius beamed. "That is *Jane Eyre*'s opening line. I see you are a reader of the classics. I encourage my agents to read them. You never know when *Little Dorritt* may be of use."

"Never mind *Little Dorritt*, who was this apparition?"

"Apparition? You object because you were kissed by a woman?" Pettigrew feigned surprise. "I am shocked, simply *shocked*. What has become of you? Where is the old Flinders, the man who doffed his hat and bowed to blushing ladies? The man who strode into lecture halls trailed by fainting students?" He clucked. "My, my, my."

"I see that you have met my assistant," Divinius said. "Her name is Gazelda—Gazelda Jones. But I call her 'point oh-three.'"

"Jones? Is she Welsh?" Flinders scowled. "Are you *sure* her name isn't Jane?"

"Not at all. The blood of Wales courses through her veins." He smiled. "She is as Welsh as the leek itself."

Lawrence was a Welshman.

"How so?"

"She has the blue eyes and the black hair."

Welshmen wander the world, Flinders thought. *They search for the far pavilions, like me. What is it about that ancient Celtic heritage? Kipling once wrote a novella,* The Man Who Would be King, *about a pair of adventurers. What drove them to claim kingship of Kafiristan? What drives Lawrence? What drives me?*

"Does she sing?" Flinders asked.

"A lovely contralto."

"A contralto?"

"She sings the lead in our agents' choir. They all sing."

Flinders imagined a dark choir. *Welshmen sing, but I suspect that they all see tigers . . . like me. And I am an Irishman.*

"Why do you call her 'point oh-three' if her name is Jones?" Flinders asked.

"It's the Dewey Decimal System. We *are* in a library, you know."

"Who is she?"

"Miss Jones is a retired witch."

"A *what?!*"

"A witch, of course."

A Welsh witch, a very bad combination.

"A witch, you say? There are no more witches," Pettigrew scoffed. "Witches have been out of fashion since the seventeenth century."

"My, my, my . . ." Divinius smiled broadly. "You *are* ill-informed. There are witches all over England." He pulled another cigarette out of a gold case and examined it. "Every day when I go for a walk, I see one."

"You see one? And every day?" Pettigrew grumbled.

"But of course."

"Let me understand." Flinders pressed the question. "You go for a walk, and you see a witch every day?"

"Obviously."

"The same witch or different witches?"

"Different witches."

"Do you greet them?" Flinders lifted an eyebrow.

"It would be impolite not to."

"Do they greet you?"

"They are most pleasant."

Pettigrew folded his hands. Mycroft smiled. The Marconi telegraph machine made noises.

"You *are* director of Intelligence here?" Pettigrew asked.

"Naturally."

"And you have a witch on your staff?"

Divinius nodded. "And rightly so."

"A singing witch."

"Witches do sing, you know."

"I'm at a loss for words." Pettigrew sighed.

"I don't see why—it's all very logical. Let me explain," Divinius said. "Miss Jones was originally in the Fabian Society and belonged to a socialist group. They carried signs and marched and generally created disturbances." He blew a large smoke ring. "But then they started reading fantasy novels. You know, books like *A Princess of Mars* or *The Worm Ouroboros* and the like. Strange stuff." He laughed. "They began to study necromancy. Then they formed a witches' coven." His eyes twinkled. "It was an easy transition, since they already believed in socialist magic. Anyway, none of their so-called spells ever worked, but at least they stopped marching."

"You must be joking," Pettigrew said.

"Not at all—England is full of strange bedfellows." Divinius smiled. "Well, one thing led to another. Gazelda decided to run for coven president. She and her followers announced that they had discovered a spell that could turn lead into gold." He leaned forward in his seat. "Alchemists had been trying for decades. The Rosicrucians almost went bankrupt. The council was ecstatic over the possibility."

Pettigrew shook his head. "I cannot believe this."

Divinius fingered his short beard. "They were to demonstrate the new spell before the coven council. It was to turn coal into gold. They used coal because they didn't have any lead." He shrugged. "Anyway, they put the coal into a large pot and boiled away. Their chanting was magnificent. The pot bubbled—something was happening. They chanted louder and danced around. The flames raged. Council members leaned forward and held their breath. Then they tilted the pot and something came out."

"What?" Flinders asked. "It couldn't possibly be . . ."

"Mud."

"Mud?"

"Yes, mud, and slippery too. It was a terrible embarrassment. A mistake in the spell." He chuckled. "There was a scene. Council members were enraged and threw shoes at them. They were stripped of their membership and sent into witches limbo. She was desperate." He smiled. "And that's when she came to me. I made her my assistant and hid her in the East Asia wing. She has a small apartment behind the Persian poetry shelves." He shook his head. "She rarely leaves the library. I'm sure you can understand."

Flinders rubbed the lip rouge off his cheek. "But still . . ."

"She's been cooped up. You are the first men she's seen in years. She may have been a little excited to meet you." Divinius stood up. "You must understand. She is an incredible asset to the Crown. She is a font of arcane knowledge. The King himself thanked her."

"And did she kiss the king?"

"No, no, no, you cannot kiss the king. The ceremony was proper and reserved." He raised his voice. "Women like Gazelda serve in silence. They may have funny code names like Pound-Worthy and the like, but they do their jobs, and without the glamor accorded handsome male agents."

"I see," Flinders said, though it was something he already knew very well to be the case.

"This unrequited service makes them a little odd at times. They yearn for field work." Divinius stood and leaned out the door. "Point oh-three, would you come in?"

Flinders looked at Pettigrew.

A grin lurked behind Pettigrew's hand.

The door opened and the figure came in. Flinders saw bright blue eyes that twinkled from behind round lenses. A cloud of dark hair circled her face. *She looks quite different in the light.*

She smiled. "Nice to meet you," she said in a husky voice.

Flinders nodded back. He did not smile.

Divinius smiled.

Pettigrew smiled.

Mycroft smiled in the portrait.

The Marconi ticked.

"Do sit down, point oh-three," Divinius told her.

She sat down. She wore a long dress and bracelets on both wrists.

"Why did you kiss me, young woman?" Flinders demanded.

"Oh, sir, you were so handsome." She smiled a shy smile. "I felt as though I was in the presence of a great hero, or perhaps even a god. I couldn't resist."

"A god, you say?"

"You are rather godlike, now that I look closer." Pettigrew grinned. "A young Zeus, perhaps, or possibly even an Adonis." He leaned in closer and peered at Flinders. "Especially with the light behind you," he added, and began whistling a few bars from *The Mikado*.

Flinders glowered. "I am not amused. And despite its popularity, I don't especially appreciate *The Mikado*. It's not one of their best."

"Flinders, sometimes you astonish me." Pettigrew clearly couldn't resist. "I would have thought that, with your wonderful baritone, you would have tried out for the role of Nanki Poo."

"Nanki Poo was a tenor, and I tried out for roles in Gilbert and Sullivan's other operas."

Gazelda folded her hands. Divinius studied his fingernails. Pettigrew studied the table. Mycroft studied the ceiling.

The Marconi chirped.

Flinders heard the faint sound of students climbing the iron stairs. A book cart wheeled by outside the door, and the librarian's shadow crossed smudged glass.

Then Divinius spoke. "Point oh-three, would you take a look at this paper?"

She took the paper, twisted it around, and held it up to the light. Then she took off her glasses, put her nose on the paper, and took an enormous sniff. Her ears wiggled with the inhalation.

Again, the sniffing: first Uncle Petrie, then Budge, and now this lady.

"Well, what do you think?"

"It's new—it doesn't smell old. Its corners are sharp, which means that it hasn't been handled by many people." She took a deep breath and smiled at Flinders. "The writing is blotchy in parts; this is a copy of an older work." She put her glasses back on. The lenses were smudged.

Flinders raised an eyebrow. "Impressive, but we already know all that. Can you tell us something that we don't know?"

Gazelda folded and unfolded the paper. Her eyes bulged behind the thick lenses. She produced a large magnifying glass and waved it back and forth. "Ah, look at this thread. See the way the gold is intertwined with the silk? It is clearly thirteenth-century Khorasani. But next to it is a plain Ottoman cotton thread." She sat back in triumph. "This weave is unique to the silk weavers of Baghdad. I would deduce that whoever used this had it made locally. Whoever wrote this is in Baghdad."

"In what quarter of the city was the paper woven?"

"Al-Attabiyah."

Pettigrew chuckled. "We missed that." He turned to Flinders. "She's good."

Flinders frowned, though his interest was piqued.

Divinius tapped ash off his cigarette.

Gazelda beamed.

"Not quite," Flinders objected. "How do you know about threads? I consider myself an expert on ancient threads, and I didn't see that."

"I read a monograph on the subject."

"Whose?"

"Yours."

Pettigrew used both hands to cover his grin. Divinius blew a smoke ring and watched it float up. Mycroft smiled down from his portrait. The Marconi made more mechanical whirring.

"Well, go on," Flinders said. "Did you find anything else?"

Gazelda fingered the paper. "Yes, there is some stitching around the edges."

"And what does that tell you?"

"The stitching is small and irregular. The paper was made by an elderly person whose hands shook."

Pettigrew stifled a cough. Divinius blew another smoke ring. It rose lazily over the table and then dissolved. Mycroft listened intently from above.

"Let me see that." Flinders took the paper. "Ah yes, the stitches are indeed small. The elderly person was a woman, no larger than seven stone." He handed the paper back. "Anything else?"

"She wore bracelets."

"On her right wrist, of course." Flinders chuckled. "The left is reserved for other purposes. But do go on."

Gazelda sniffed again. "There is a strong smell of hashish, probably from the person who carried it. I have had some experience with hashish."

"No doubt you have."

Divinius held the cigarette to his head. "I have occasionally taken hashish." He smiled. "For medicinal purposes only, of course. You have no idea how hard on the back it is to read Intelligence reports all day."

Flinders found himself becoming impatient. "Anything else?"

"There is another scent: Turkish cigarettes. Someone else smoked Turkish cigarettes."

"Turkish cigarettes, is it?" Pettigrew twiddled a paper in front of him.

Divinius put his cigarette out and stared at the stub.

"Give that to me." Flinders smelled the paper. "The cigarette smell is pronounced—it was on his hands. The Veiled One is a heavy smoker." *Now they've got me sniffing*, he thought.

"Can you tell what brand?" Gazelda's lenses looked innocent.

Flinders smiled. "Fatima."

"Possibly Istanbul Blue instead?" Gazelda offered.

The lenses twinkled.

The woman has a nose like a bloodhound.

Divinius contemplated his cigarette case; Pettigrew inspected his nails. Flinders took another sniff. *Who is this terrible woman?*

Steps clunked on the iron stairs. Faint laughter floated in. The Marconi stopped whirring with a *pop*. Mycroft smiled down. Father Divinius broke in. "I smoke Egyptian Deities, myself."

"Thank you for that." Flinders waved the paper. "But I detect more. There is a wine scent."

"Wine?" The lenses-wearing woman smiled. "I love wine."

"Of course, you do," Pettigrew said. "It goes wonderfully with hashish."

Flinders waved the vellum. "The Veiled One took a glass of wine before he handed the paper to the hashshashin. He drinks French wine." Flinders smiled broadly at Gazelda and folded his arms.

"But what varietal?"

"What do you mean, 'what varietal?'"

"I can identify the varietal."

"No doubt from guzzling wine at your many incantations," Flinders said, smoothing his hair and handing over the vellum. "But if you insist."

"I do." She sniffed again. "It's a blend from Bordeaux."

"Mycroft was fond of Bordeaux blends." Divinius looked up at the portrait. "We shared many a glass at the Diogenes."

"What vineyard?"

This woman is rapidly becoming infuriating. Yet there is something enchanting about her, even.

Flinders took the paper back, sniffed it again, and then thought for a moment. "To the north. Chateau Ausone, I think." Flinders steepled his hands. "The Veiled One has excellent taste."

"Are you sure? I think perhaps Chateau Lynch-Bages."

"Yes, I am sure. The wine has no water taste, therefore the grapes were grown on a hillside with little moisture. Lynch-Bages's vines are on a flatter and wetter plain."

Why am I discussing vineyards with this person?

Flinders thought a moment.

She wears perfume. Mystere, I think. Why should such a woman wear perfume that speaks of allure and adventure? Does she dream of

*far pavilions, like I do? Or does she dream about something more inti-
mate? I need to think about this, but, in the meantime, she is a terrible
nuisance.*

Pettigrew and Divinius looked at each other.

"If I may be so bold," Divinius began, glancing up at the portrait
of Mycroft, "your consensus is that the firman was made in Baghdad,
and you suspect that the Veiled One may be there also."

Both Flinders and Gazelda nodded.

"I think that corresponds to our opinion as well." Divinius smiled,
Mycroft smiled, and the Marconi clattered in approval.

"Well, that settles it," Pettigrew said. "We must go to Baghdad. The
relic may still be there."

*That settles nothing. Now they are going to insist that this, this . . .
whatever this woman is, go with us. I can feel it coming. But either way,
go we must.*

"I will cable Princess Badroulbadour in our Baghdad office."

"Princess Badroulbadour?" Flinders said.

"Yes, of course." Divinius smiled. "Aladdin married her after he
found the magic lamp."

"I am confused." Flinders shook his head. "How is it that we are
discussing Aladdin?"

"And who, may I ask, is Princess Badroulbadour?"

"Why, Gertrude Bell, of course. That is her code name."

Gertrude of the green eyes. "Ah, the redoubtable Miss Bell." Flinders
chuckled. "No doubt she will be delighted to see us."

Pettigrew looked at the files.

"Thomas, you have a princess waiting for you."

Pettigrew was noncommittal.

"I suppose that the Kalendar Prince is there as well?"

"No, no, no, the Kalendar Prince is in Damascus."

"And Sinbad?" Flinders persisted.

"In Basrah, where else?"

"I dread to think where Ali Baba is."

"In Hadhramaut."

"Hadhramaut?"

"The home of frankincense and myrrh."

"So let me understand this." Flinders grinned. "Badroulbadour is in Baghdad."

"Yes."

"The Kalendar Prince is in Damascus."

"Exactly so." Divinius beamed.

"And Sinbad is in Hadhramaut." Flinders leaned back in triumph.

"No, Sinbad is in Basrah."

Flinders shrugged. "All right, Ali Baba is in Hadhramaut."

"The home of frankincense and myrrh."

"I have it, then."

"Correct." Divinius clapped his hands. "Mycroft arranged for all this. He thought that it would add a touch of elegance and romance to our operation."

"Wait." Flinders leaned forward.

"Yes?" Divinius pulled his glasses down.

"Where is Aladdin?"

"You have a mind like a steel trap, sir." Divinius frowned. "But I cannot tell you."

"Why not?"

"Because his whereabouts are a secret."

"I should have guessed."

Pettigrew buried his head in his arms.

"But about Baghdad—"

"Marvelous place. Scheherazade still lurks there."

"Another agent?" Flinders asked.

"No, no, no, just a figure of speech."

Flinders persisted. "Never mind that—how are we going to wander around Baghdad unnoticed?"

Divinius thought a moment. His cigarette ash burned a hole in the file before him. "You will need a disguise, if you plan to move around freely."

Flinders smiled. "We had thought of traveling as priests."

"An excellent idea." Divinius laughed. "No one pays any attention to priests these days. There is a store in London that sells clerical clothing. I will provide you with certificates—you can't just walk in and buy a priest's outfit." He paused. "I think you should go as Greek Orthodox. They are relatively noncontroversial in the area, and the Ottomans have granted them substantial autonomy. They control their own communities."

He rummaged around in a drawer. Cigarette ashes fell in the papers in it. "Just tell the salesman that you want Greek number three."

"Greek number three?"

"Yes. Greek number one is the Patriarch. Greek number two is a Metropolitan. And Greek number three is an ordinary priest," Divinius rumbled. "And don't let them sell you solid gold chains and accoutrements either—gold plate is good enough."

Flinders grinned. "Do they have tailors?"

"No, you will be wearing cassocks." Divinius stroked his beard. "Of course, you will have to grow beards." He stopped mid-thought. "I don't suppose either of you speak Greek."

"No," Pettigrew answered.

Divinius looked disappointed.

"Wait," Gazelda interrupted. "I can go along and translate. I speak Greek. I had to learn it to cast spells."

"Spells. But of course you did," Flinders scoffed.

"Don't be so snippy." Pettigrew grinned. "I seem to remember that once you were planning to become a necromancer." He leaned back in his chair. "Yes, you said that you were in communication with Doctor Mesmer himself, impossible as that seems. We were about to enter a tomb, and I had to beg you not to become 'magical.'"

"That was years ago."

"Years ago, indeed."

"Anyway, I read and speak some Greek. I might be rusty, but I'm sure it will come back." Flinders smiled. "As I said, I am a classical scholar."

"I think Miss Jones will do admirably." Pettigrew grinned.

I knew it. Flinders glowered at Pettigrew. "Look, we can't take a woman into a war zone. Since the fall of the sultan, the whole place is in chaos."

"I imagine she can take care of herself."

"You think so, do you? By chanting and casting spells?"

"I think you might be pleasantly surprised," Pettigrew insisted.

"You are quite right," Divinius said. "Miss Jones is indeed formidable."

Formidable, indeed. She will drive me insane, wobbling about all over, mumbling incantations.

Gazelda shook her head; her dark curls bobbled enthusiastically.

Flinders rolled his eyes.

Divinius nodded. "She has taken all the courses and passed all the examinations for field agent. And she has spent many hours at pistol practice over in the Greco-Roman wing. She can nick the target off a marble hand without injuring its fingers. She has a license to kill, you know—actual field work might be just the thing."

License to kill, is it? Field work, is it? Divinius should keep her locked up in the Roman wing. Then she could shoot at all the emperors she could find.

Divinius turned to Gazelda. "You've been stuck here too long. Let me think. Yes, you could go as an acolyte. I will arrange it."

An acolyte? Will wonders never cease?

Gazelda beamed again. Pettigrew and Divinius smiled.

Flinders shook his head and frowned. *Now what am I to do?* "You're not going to cast spells and make trouble, are you?" he grumbled. "No wands, understand?"

"Oh, no, sir." She pulled the glasses down her nose and looked over them with wide, innocent eyes. "I gave up wands years ago."

No wands—a small victory. But I feel like Napoleon after Waterloo.

So the deed was done, much to Flinders's displeasure. He now found himself in the company of a wild-looking woman with a mind like a straight razor. And he knew that he would soon be face to face with an implacable enemy. Flinders shook his head, and his mind traveled back. *The Apostles walked the Middle East, across deserts and mountains to bring the Word. Now we must follow the same route to prevent a catastrophe.*

"All right, let's pack. We will have to take a steamer through the Canal and into the Red Sea, and then to the Persian Gulf and Basrah." He turned to Gazelda. "I hope you are not susceptible to seasickness."

"I'm sorry, but I am."

I could have guessed. Now I will have to carry around a seasick witch.

☙

They took the train from Oxford. Pettigrew wrapped himself in a blanket. Gazelda stared out the compartment window. Flinders buried his head in a book.

Pettigrew snored.

"What are you reading?" Gazelda tried to make conversation.

"*The Lives of the Saints.*" Flinders looked up. "It seems appropriate."

"I once read the biography of Saint Genevieve."

"Of course, you did." Flinders closed his book. "And I hope you found it instructive."

The remainder of the trip was completed in strained silence.

Finally, Flinders thought as the train rolled into the station. *At least there were no tigers.* He stood up and reached for the valises. *But the tiger paces in my mind, and its stripes burn in the forest of my night.*

The station smelled of soot. Steam engines hooted and shuffled in and out on shining tracks. The sun blazed between iron awnings and covered gray trains with dusty light. Crowds of passengers milled about. Conductors shouted, "All aboard!" and waved their lanterns. Flinders watched a red baggage cart carrying his belongings roll away down the long platform. They followed it. "Come on, the cabs are this way." Pettigrew pushed Flinders down the platform. "Stop lagging, we have to get to the docks."

☙

They boarded the steamer at Southampton. Flinders stowed his luggage in a cabin and then went out on deck. Lines of deck chairs greeted him. *I once set sail for Cairo. I was younger then and the world was bright. Now I am older, and the world does not seem so bright.*

Crowded docks slid past.

Wind ruffled his hair, seagulls circled above him, and salt air swirled in his nostrils. Pettigrew and Gazelda smiled beside him. Flinders closed his eyes. *We sail into the Roman past. Will its violence destroy us? But this was what I wanted.* The ship's motion relaxed him, and his thoughts wandered. *The Roman legions marched in precision. Curled trumpets brayed their implacable approach. The thump of their feet was the sound of doom. The Christians watched them with horror. Women cried and children wailed.*

A horn blast brought light and sound back. The legions faded into the empty past, and the sound of their trumpets dissolved into dust.

Flags waved, and the crowd cheered as the ship cleared the harbor.

Flinders shook his head and looked at the empty deck chairs. "This time there are no young ladies to smile at me." He chuckled. "I miss the outraged aunts."

THREE

The Ghost of Scheherazade

Flinders smiled when he came on deck. He looked down the rows of bare teak and then out at the sea. "There are no lovely ladies, but the scene is beautiful all the same."

Sparkling foam flowed past the steamer's hull. The sea was a bright blue strip between the arid brown of the land. Nothing moved on either side of the steamer. The soft chug of the engines was the only sound. Flinders leaned over the rail and studied the green emptiness. A fish jumped out of the gentle waves, then another, and another. Their bodies glittered before him. The sun blazed in the bright sky; he pulled his hat brim down. High above, a desert hawk wheeled black in the brightness. He heard its faint shriek echoing through the clear air.

It cries high above me in the clear desert air. It circles and circles endlessly. What do those circles mean? Am I like that hawk, searching, searching, always searching?

A cabin door opened behind him, and he turned to look. Gazelda came out. She wore a khaki trench coat that fell to her ankles, a large hat whose brim covered her face, and blue saucers across her nose.

"Why are you dressed like that?" Flinders stared at the apparition. "It is hotter than Hades out here."

"I sunburn easily."

"Of course you do." Flinders frowned. "I should have known. You have spent a long time in the basement of the Ashmolean."

"It's not that," Gazelda said. "I was a forward on the ladies' lacrosse team, so I saw a great deal of sunlight. But I still get sunburned."

"A lacrosse-playing witch. My, my, my . . ." Flinders smiled. "Did you use a lacrosse stick or a wand?"

The saucers frowned.

Flinders chuckled.

She came to the rail beside him and gripped it with both hands.

"Are you all right?"

"I'm fine."

"You're not going to fall overboard, are you?" Flinders smiled slightly. "You look a little wobbly."

"I am not wobbly."

"Can you swim?"

"No."

"I thought not. Witches generally sink when placed in water."

"It's not that. I just never learned."

"From what I can see of you, you look a little green."

"I am quite all right, thank you." She looked at the sea. "Where are we?"

"We're about to leave the Red Sea." Flinders pointed to his left. "We have entered the Bab al-Mandeb, the Gate of Tears. Over there is Aqaba, with its Ottoman garrison. You can't really see it in the haze. The Turks have fortified it. Their guns control the end of the Red Sea."

Lawrence told me about Aqaba that night in Carchemish. He said that it controlled the sea route but that its guns pointed away from the desert. He smiled and said that if he were organizing a military operation, he would charge it from the desert. His eyes glowed as he described the charge. The green flag of the prophet floated behind him. The riders screamed "Allahu Akbar" as they spurred on their camels; their hooves thrummed the sand and the desert shook beneath them. His machine pistol chattered in the morning air.

Sparkling waves rolled in front of him, and salt air bit his lungs. *But then, do not all of us imagine such things?* He leaned over the railing. *At night, when we are about to slide into sleep, do we not all imagine ourselves as kings, or dukes, or lovers? And does not this flight of imagination allow us to get up in the cold morning and face the world anew?*

The evening was late, and the fire burned low. Woolley, Pettigrew, and Gertrude had left. Lawrence fixed me with his eyes and said, "All men dream, but not equally. Those who dream at night awake to find nothing but emptiness. But those who dream by day may act on those dreams to make them possible."

Am I such a dreamer?

"The Gate of Tears? What does that mean?"

Gazelda's question jarred him into the present. The sea was again bright in the sun.

"Herodotus tells us that an ancient earthquake separated Africa from the Arabian Peninsula. Thousands were killed. The lamentations lasted for years."

The Gate of Tears. Am I about to enter a time of lamentations? The sea was bright in his eyes. *The sea shines, but my mind is dark and I am uneasy. . . . The emissary said it was the world of the sword. I am uneasy, indeed. The Gate of Tears may mean exactly what its name implies, yet I am compelled to come.*

The flutter of a large hat ended his reverie.

Flinders turned to her. All he could see was the tip of a nose. "Tell me about yourself," he said. "How did you manage to become a witch?"

The blue saucers regarded him thoughtfully. "My parents died when I was very young, and I was sent to an orphanage. The owners of the orphanage were very cruel to me. Sometimes they would lock me up in an unused room as punishment."

"An unused room?"

The blue saucers fogged. "The room was bare and cold. I was afraid."

"Afraid?"

"Yes. I imagined there was someone else in the room that I could not see." She looked up at Flinders. "Have you ever been afraid of something you know is there, but you cannot see it?"

"Yes, all the time."

The tiger stalks me. A flash of fire here, the glow of stripes there.

She nodded.

"So you are a modern-day Jane Eyre?"

"Who was Jane Eyre?"

"Someone very like you." *Or someone very like me*, Flinders thought. *Am I Rochester, condemned to a hell of my own making? The yellow eyes glow. The tiger glides toward me. I cannot move. I can see it in my mind, but I cannot see it with my eyes.*

Flinders grinned. "I would have thought that you read everything the Brontës wrote. You seem like someone who would be entranced by Gothic horror. Perhaps *Frankenstein* is more to your liking."

She shook her head. "I read *Wuthering Heights* and decided I didn't like Heathcliff, so I never read anything else by them." She smiled. "They were very odd, you know."

"Very odd indeed. Some say that Heathcliff and Catherine were both really vampires. But of course, they were just merely very unpleasant people. Please do go on."

"The orphanage had a large hall with a window. I would sit on the window seat and read fairy tales."

Flinders closed his eyes. *The window is large; the girl is small. She has long black braids. She sits and holds a large book, her glasses drooping down her nose. She turns the pages with rapt attention.*

"Fairy tales?"

"I used to dream that someday a handsome prince would rescue me."

"Handsome princes are in short supply these days."

"I would look out the window. There was nothing but brick walls and broken shutters." She brushed a stray curl back under her hat. "But I would imagine that they were the walls of a fairy castle, all airy and white, with pennants streaming from the high towers. And beautiful people dressed in silks, walking and laughing."

She adjusted her glasses.

"Then trumpets would sound and a prince on a white charger would come riding at the head of a parade of attendants. He would lean over his mighty horse and scoop me up and carry me across the drawbridge."

A prince on a mighty charger. We all dream of princes on mighty chargers. And sometimes we dream that we are that prince. "Mighty chargers make the earth tremble," he said.

She pulled an ear and sighed. "And I would live happily ever after."

The steamer's horn sounded. Sea spray blew across the deck. Flinders turned to her. "Fairy castles are the best kind," he told her.

"But it never happened. Each day was the same as every other day." She leaned over the rail. "Then, one morning, I got out of bed and dressed. It was still dark out, and nobody was up. I slipped down the stairs and opened the front door."

"And then?"

"And then I ran away and joined a circus."

"Circuses are not friendly places."

I remember a circus. The car stopped beside a wall; its wipers thumped.

The circus posters were wrinkled from the rain and the freaks' distorted faces grimaced out, their wide grins potent with malevolence.

"I made friends with the freaks. The bearded lady was my roommate. In a way, I felt like one of them. I felt at home."

"You made friends with the freaks?"

"Yes." She sighed. "They were all terribly deformed, but I loved them anyway."

Flinders remembered a baby. The desert was bright, the tents were black silhouettes against the brightness, and the baby felt warm. A boy, his face was red and wrinkled, and his eyes were closed. *He snuggled against my chest. And then he was gone.*

"Interesting."

"At first, the ringmaster didn't know what to do with me. He said, 'You are our Cinderella, but we do not have a prince, and you do not have glass slippers.' So he set me to groom the animals. Every morning, I would brush the ponies."

Flinders's mind drifted. *A young girl walks into a paddock. The morning sun is bright; the circus tents are white. The ponies crowd around her; she carries a bucket of grain. The ponies poke their noses into the bucket. She laughs and pushes them away.*

The blue saucers smiled. "I loved brushing the ponies. There was an old mare named Molly. She was brown with a white mane that stretched to her forelegs. She loved ear scratches. She would follow me around asking for more. She would whinny and bump me with her head." The saucers dimmed. "Then, one day, they took her away. The ringmaster said, 'She's too old to do tricks.' Sometimes, I wonder if that will happen to me."

We all wonder about that.

A gust of wind blew her hat off and it skittered along the deck. Flinders sprinted after it and caught it on the bounce. He presented it to her with a grin. "Miss Jones, your hat."

She giggled and pulled it down even farther across her nose.

"Then what happened?"

"Then the magician said, 'I need an assistant.'"

"A magician?"

"Yes, the circus had a magician. So I became a magician's assistant."

Flinders laughed. "I wanted to become a magician once. I once tried to correspond with Doctor Mesmer. He had been dead for seventy years, but I thought that if I read everything he wrote, our minds would meet. I wanted to enter the realm of the subconscious and do magical things." Flinders paused. "I understand. Go on."

"I worked for the great Thurstan. He was American, but he ran away and joined a circus in England. He was magnificent. He had curly black hair and a huge mustache."

"I know of him. I practiced his magic tricks."

The blue saucers smiled. "He once said to me, 'We are both runaways, so we have to be good magicians.'"

"I have seen his playbills."

"I helped him set up the show, and then I would be his assistant onstage. I loved acting."

I once pushed a mummy onstage—the cart wheels squeaked. The audience applauded.

"We became friends. I used to call him 'Thursty.'"

"But of course you did."

The blue saucers twinkled. "He once made an entire pub full of Irishmen disappear."

"How so?"

"He shouted, 'The Temperance ladies are coming, and they are bringing your wives.' In a second, the pub was empty except for one old man and his dog. 'I'm not married,' he said. 'Bartender, another whiskey, and a beer for my dog.'"

Flinders hid a smile behind his hand. *She is better than Pettigrew.*

"I studied with the great Thurstan and learned sleight of hand. Do you want to see?"

"Of course." How could he resist such an invitation?

She took out a fifty-piaster coin and held it in one hand. "Watch," she said. She turned both hands over and then turned the palms up. "Now you see it, now you don't." Both hands were empty.

"Impressive. Now give me that." He took the coin in one hand with the tips of his fingers and then slid it slowly into his palm. "Gone."

He opened an empty hand.

The blue saucers were astonished. "How did you do that?"

"At Oxford, I took a tutorial in the art of sleight of hand, and later I wrote a monograph on it." Flinders grinned. "You must have missed it in your research." He handed her the coin. "Perhaps with more practice . . ."

The blue saucers scowled.

She scowls at me. There is a strange excitement about her presence. Interesting.

They leaned over the rail and studied the azure water flowing under the steamer's prow. A fish jumped from the sparkling foam. Brilliant crystals of water drenched them. Gazelda shook her hands. "I am soaked."

"So you are." Flinders brushed water from his arms. "But at least you did not hiss and disappear in a puff of smoke. There may be hope for you yet."

The saucers frowned.

Heat curled up from the deck. The oak planking became sticky as its varnish melted. The iron railing blistered their hands. "Your nose is getting sunburned," Flinders said. He reached into a pocket and pulled out a small bottle. "Here, I have some ointment." *Maggie was always worrying about our sunburn when we came back from the Middle East. She would make us stand still while she clucked and slathered us with goo.*

"Hold still."

They leaned over the rail, shoulder to shoulder. No one spoke. The sea foamed green and blue before them. The sun was hot on their backs; the spray was cold in their faces. After a while, both went to their cabins. Flinders watched her go in. The cabin door clicked shut behind her. *She's beginning to grow on me. There is a softness to her. There was magic on that deck.* Then he rubbed his chin and grumbled, "A softness like some exotic plague."

Fairy castles, indeed. He slammed the cabin door.

Seagulls circled lazily overhead. The steamer slid into the harbor at Basrah and edged its way down a corridor of high-sterned feluccas, their slanted sails tinged red by the setting sun and their dark masts fingers of black reaching for the sky. Flinders watched as a forest of masts and stacks floated past. The smell of fish was everywhere. He could see a line of palm trees on the approaching shore. A humid breeze warmed his face. He turned to Gazelda.

"This is where Sinbad began his voyages."

Passengers trundled down the gangway; baggage carts rumbled by. Hawkers shouted their wares, and beggars reached out. Pettigrew pushed them through the crowd and into an open carriage pulled by one horse. He handed the driver a note in Arabic. "We will stay the night at the Saint Regis," he said, once they were settled inside the carriage. "Divinius said that an agent would meet us there and arrange for a car to take us to Baghdad."

The carriage jolted off through a jungle of carts, animals, and people. Men in striped gallabiyahs and women in black cluttered the horse's way. Some women carried babies; some led children by the hand.

Gazelda stared at the black shapes. "They all look alike," she said.

"But they are not all alike," Flinders said. "Each wears her burka differently. Their husbands and relatives can identify them instantly by the way they carry themselves."

"So now you are an anthropologist?" Pettigrew said.

"After we came back from Cairo, I attended some lectures by Professor Durkheim. His comments on social interaction were most instructive." Flinders paused, shaking his head. "Thomas, once you said something about how we supposedly civilized men have lost the ability to relate to each other." He looked at the passing women. "Whatever they are, they can relate to each other."

Gazelda shuddered. "But the babies have flies around their eyes."

"They are fruit flies. They stick to babies' faces and carry disease and blindness. The mothers do what they can to brush them off," Pettigrew responded. "I am a physician—I will tell you about disease and infant death. Flinders is a poet—he will tell you about Sinbad and Ali Baba and the glories of the *Arabian Nights*."

"But which vision is true?" she asked.

"Both," Pettigrew said.

Flinders nodded. "Someone once explained that the universe turns left here."

"Yes," Pettigrew added. "The universe turns left. Men in white whirl in search of God."

"And do they find God?"

"I do not know. I am only an Englishman."

The carriage bumped and swayed. Rows of striped awnings passed over their heads, and flickering shafts of sun and shade crossed their faces as the carriage drove forward. Tables overflowing with fruit and vegetables swam by. Piles of melons spilled into the street and stacks of round loaves ringed the carriage. Hawkers pushed bracelets and neck-laces out. Small boys clutched the sides of the carriage and begged for bakshish. Flinders opened his collar and took off his coat; the back of his shirt was wet. The air smelled of spices and cooking meat.

The horse reared up and its eyes rolled; the driver reined it in. The crowd grew quiet and shrank away from the street. Hawkers put down their wares. The small boys stood still. Awnings swayed in the breeze. The street was silent except for the muffed sound of walking feet and the click of hooves on the cobbles.

A long line of women and children crossed in front of the carriage, their backs bent with despair. There were one or two old men, some boys, but no young women. They carried bundles of belongings. A trail of dropped belongings marked the line's path. The women's long skirts were dusty. Some of the children cried; others laughed. One small girl had a pet cat curled around her neck. Horsemen in gray prodded the women with long sticks. A woman staggered and fell to her knees; an elderly man tried to help her. He stumbled. The horsemen beat them until they got back up.

"Armini." The driver turned in his seat and shook his head.

A small boy kicked the dirt as he walked; his mother cried. A girl in blue gingham waved at the stopped carriage. Her face was smudged with dirt.

Gazelda waved back. "Where are they going?"

The driver frowned and drew a finger across his neck.

"To their execution?" Gazelda started crying.

"There are no young women." Flinders stared at the line. "Where are the young women?"

The driver shook his head. "Turk harem."

"As slaves, or worse," Pettigrew said. He clenched his jaw.

Flinders watched them disappear into a side street. His eyes clouded. *They are like figures out of an ancient past. We return to the terrors of the first century. The Christians sang as they were crucified. Hammers pounded nails into their hands. They screamed in agony and then began singing. The screams and singing faded. The night became dark along the Appian Way. Figures of burning Christians shed smoky flames into the night. Their heads lolled in death. The smell of burning flesh and tar was everywhere. And now it begins again.*

But what am I to do?

Dull thuds brought Flinders back to the heat and stench of Basrah. Another old woman had fallen. The line passed slowly. Crowds closed around the path of grief as though nothing had happened. Small boys picked up the fallen bundles and darted away with their prizes.

This is how it must have happened centuries ago. Christians were marched to their deaths. Everybody watched, but nobody did anything to stop the execution. Now, it happens again. The Armenians march, the soldiers beat them, but nobody does anything.

Pettigrew closed his eyes.

"I cannot watch," Gazelda said and covered her face.

The driver stared straight ahead.

No, you must watch. You must see with open eyes.

The sad procession passed, and the driver snapped his whip.

The street filled again with black figures. Babies cried. Carts rumbled, and hawkers touted their wares.

Then they were gone, as though they had never existed.

The carriage jolted forward and clattered through the crowded streets. It finally stopped in front of an imposing bronze door—the Saint Regis. A doorman in a white kaftan bowed and opened it. Flinders got out of the carriage, followed by Pettigrew and Gazelda, and the three of them entered the lobby. A sea of red velvet and gold greeted him.

After what I have just seen, all the magnificence in the world could not cleanse my mind. Still, he attempted to remain buoyant, saying, "This reminds me of the Pera Palace." He studied the lobby. "I can still remember wobbling down the main staircase the morning after drinking all night with Kudret."

"I can already feel the headache," Pettigrew said, nodding.

"Then we had to face Gertrude."

"She was not pleased."

Flinders looked at the floor. "Your woman had a tongue like a snake."

"Indeed, she did." Pettigrew laughed. "She was merciless that morning. 'Do you like your gin with garlic?' she said. 'The ambassador always had garlic with his gin.' I still shudder at the thought." Gertrude's green eyes had bored into his. "I remember her saying, 'We must be alert, Mr. Petrie. The great Sherlock Holmes was always alert.'"

Flinders smiled to himself. *Yes, the great Holmes was always alert. What would he see in this place?*

His eyes swept the lobby as he approached the front desk. The medallioned carpet was dusty. A few wilted palms sat in large jars. The air smelled of stale cigarette smoke. A clerk in brown sat in front of a line of cubbyholes. Some had keys hanging out, some had letters, and others were empty. A cat stretched on a bench and licked its paws. Nothing seemed to move. Soldiers in gray uniforms lounged in corners, their rifles leaned against the walls. A few men sat in velvet chairs. Cigarette smoke drifted above their heads. One read a newspaper in English; it was upside-down.

The desk clerk said something in Arabic and held out his hand.

Flinders looked at Pettigrew. "He wants to see your papers."

A tall man in a fez had appeared from nowhere. He leaned over the counter next to Flinders's elbow. "We are very concerned about spies here." He smelled of strong cologne, and a zigzag scar ran down his jaw.

Flinders smiled. "Of course," he said and handed the papers to the clerk. The clerk shuffled through them and frowned. The soldiers rustled. The reading man folded his newspaper. Then the clerk looked at the tall man and nodded.

The clerk said something else.

"Englishmen," the tall man said. "What brings you to our little city?"

"We're on a tour of the monuments in Iraq," Flinders said. "I teach archaeology classes."

"And these," the tall man said, frowning and pointing to Pettigrew and Gazelda, "are your assistants?"

The soldiers picked up their rifles.

"No, no," Flinders said. "They are friends and amateur archaeologists."

"Amateur archaeologists, is it?" The tall man stared at Gazelda and mumbled something to himself.

The smokers stood up from their chairs.

Gazelda smiled and then pulled a dog-eared copy of Layard's *Nineveh and Its Remains* out of a large bag. "I have been reading this," she said breathlessly. "These ruins are magnificent." She pulled her glasses down and looked over them with wide blue eyes. "Perhaps you have seen them?"

"No, I have not." The tall man managed a tight smile. "I am sure that you will enjoy them."

Flinders arched an eyebrow in Gazelda's direction. *Well played. A little dicey perhaps, but still well played.*

The clerk asked another question.

"He wants to know if you are Armenian," the tall man said. He wore a black suit. His lips were thin, and his face was pockmarked. Flinders saw uneven stubble on his cheeks. He did not smile.

"We are not." Flinders grinned and smoothed his hair. "I am Irish to the core." He mugged at the tall man.

"Let me look," the tall man insisted. "No, your noses are wrong."

The smokers sat down.

If he had said that to Cyrano, he would have been dead on the spot.

"Wait." The tall man looked at Gazelda. "You may be Assyrian. There are many Assyrians in Basrah. Please take off your glasses."

The scar gleamed white as he turned his head back and forth, and his eyes became slits of darkness.

Flinders nodded. *Now let's see what she does.*

A clock chimed in a distant hallway; the chimes reverberated in the silence. The tall man slowly searched Gazelda's face. Cigarette smoke curled up from the velvet chairs.

"No, your eyes are too blue." The tall man smiled a tight smile again. "Assyrians have brown eyes."

That was close. Mariam had gray eyes.

The tall man said something to the clerk. "You may go. We will send your luggage to your room." The clerk handed Flinders some keys and pointed to a Rococo staircase with gilded banisters. "Your rooms are on the second floor," the tall man said.

The soldiers relaxed. The reading man lit a cigarette. Rifle butts clicked on the floor. Cigarette smoke drifted across the lobby.

"Have a nice stay."

Flinders smiled. "Thank you, we will." He turned, pushed them toward the stairs, and muttered under his breath, "Turkish cigarettes smell terrible. Why don't they smoke Pall Malls?"

They climbed the ornate staircase to the second floor. "Faster, Miss Jones," Flinders whispered as he pushed them to the second floor. "That man's tailoring was atrocious." He sniffed. "And that cologne . . . my, my, my." He glanced behind. "They are watching us." They reached the landing and walked down the dim hall; floorboards creaked under their steps. Silent doors with tattered room service tags slid past. A forlorn maid's cart blocked their way; its sheets and towels drooped listlessly.

Flinders turned to Gazelda. "Wait. How is it that you brought a copy of *Nineveh* with you?"

The glasses twinkled. "Joseph Bell always said that a detective should always be prepared."

"Joseph Bell said *that*, did he?" Flinders scowled. "And how is it that you know Joseph Bell?"

"I studied with Professor Bell. He was retired, but he corresponded with me and sent me all of his lectures."

"Really?"

"Yes, and he remembered you."

"He remembered me?"

"He said that you were one of his brightest students but a little wild. He hoped that you would settle down and become more professional."

"More professional?"

"Yes, he said that you needed more seasoning." She pulled her glasses down, and her bright blue eyes twinkled as she turned to fully face him. "Actually, he said you were somewhat scattered."

"Scattered?"

Why do I talk to this woman? Flinders shook his head and continued walking.

Nothing moved; the hall was soundless. The faded red carpet stretched to a dusty infinity. Bare bulbs lit their way, some of them burned out. Flinders surveyed the hallway. "I do not think that we will have a 'nice stay.'"

A man stepped out of the shadow. A long kufiyah covered part of his face.

He uncovered his face. "Tomorrow, you leave for Baghdad. Get up early and eat a good breakfast—there will be no food in the car. Get up early, before the police change shifts. The ones that stay up all night will be too sleepy to notice you. Leave your luggage in the room. We will move it to the car."

He twisted the kufiyah. "The last part of the journey will be at night. There are patrols. When you hear the call to prayer, you can leave the hotel and turn left. The car will be waiting. Its headlights are painted blue. Maa Salamah." He vanished into the gloom.

Divinius has a long reach, thought Flinders.

Three room doors clicked open. The rooms smelled of dry must and cleaning fluid; shades covered their windows. It was clear no one had been here for a long time. Flinders threw himself on a dusty bed. Its springs squeaked and its mattress was hard.

Have a nice stay, *indeed*.

Breakfast was short. Early morning sun shone through the dining room's tall windows; its rays bounced off the white tile floor. The dining room was empty except for the three. Most of the tables were bare and had no chairs. Three sleepy waiters moved silently about, their eyes guarded. "We're being watched," Flinders whispered from behind his napkin. "Act normal, and smile." He grinned at Gazelda. "Be cheerful."

The waiter set plates of hummus and eggs in front of them. Flinders looked up from his plate. "Have you ever eaten hummus before, Miss Jones?"

Gazelda shook her head.

Pettigrew took a bite and then stared into space for a long moment.

"Thomas eats hummus nearly every day," Flinders continued. "Once, our old housekeeper tried to add roasted vegetables to it, but Thomas objected. He wanted it to be like the hummus in Cairo." Flinders smiled. "Memories, you know. So don't just pick at your food, Miss Jones—we are supposed to be on a fun tour of the city."

Flinders raised his cup to signal the waiter. The waiter poured coffee. Flinders saw his hand shake slightly. He seemed to be afraid of something.

Flinders finished the cup and forced a smile. "That coffee was quite good. I do believe I will have another cup. This is quite pleasant—the morning sun warms my shoulders. I may sit here all morning."

Gazelda twisted her napkin and glared at him.

Pettigrew grinned. "Sometimes he likes to demonstrate his aplomb."

Out of the corner of his eye, Flinders saw the waiters begin to shift uneasily. "Everyone done?" He folded his napkin into a neat square—an old habit—and then stared at it. "It's time to go."

They stood up and went into the lobby; cigarette smoke curled up as before.

"Now, we must tour the town," Flinders said in a loud voice as he opened a thick red *Baedeker's* guide. "Ah, first we should visit the old city and see the famous Shanasheel porches." He turned the pages. "It says here that they are magnificent examples of Islamic wood carving. Come along." He nodded to the waiters and pushed Pettigrew and Gazelda out of the dining room.

They crossed the lobby. Flinders smiled at the desk clerk and loudly read from the *Baedeker's*. He hoped it sounded convincing. "And after that, we shall take a boat ride up the Shatt al-Arab." They slid past the dozing men in the velvet chairs. Cigarette butts covered the medallioned carpet. A rumpled newspaper fluttered in the breeze from the overhead fans. The soldiers had disappeared; their rifles leaned against a wall. Flinders saw the tall man watching from a corner behind the front desk and muttered to himself, "His tailoring looks even worse in the light of day."

The hotel's bronze door closed behind them, and Flinders waved hello to the doorman. Moist heat slapped him in the face, and as he stepped onto the rough pavement, he saw two men in gray suits lounging against the hotel wall.

"Let me look." Flinders unfolded a map from the *Baedeker's* and peered at it. "Yes, this way, I think." He pointed to his left. "Mind you don't trip, Miss Jones—the pavement is uneven."

He felt the men in gray watching them as they walked away.

The car with the blue headlights waited in the morning sun. The driver beckoned. They tumbled in; the seats were already hot. The engine coughed to a start.

❧

The morning desert was alive with lambent light. "An opal, indeed," Flinders said, recalling Gertrude's words. *She was right*, he thought.

She had said something else at Carchemish: "See the desert in a fine morning and die—if you can."

The opal quickly grew into intense brightness. The car sped across emptiness. Nothing moved. Flinders lolled in the back seat. Pettigrew dozed beside him. Gazelda's head drooped over the front seat. Pale brown haze blurred into a gray horizon. A few insects spattered on the windscreen. The track became rougher, and the car slowed to a crawl. A solitary camel trotted behind the slow-moving car for a few miles and then wandered off into the desert.

Flinders pulled his neckerchief over his nose. His open collar was wet with sweat.

Solitary bedouin on camels passed by, heads bowed, riding listlessly in the dust. As the car drew abreast of them, Flinders said, "Remind you of Nellie, Thomas?"

"No. Nellie always pranced."

"Camels don't prance."

"Nellie did."

The searing sun turned into an angry red orb and sank behind the horizon. The red glow spread slowly across the desert and then disappeared. The moon rose, a half circle of white. But Flinders could see its full circle outlined against the stars. Moonlight turned the desert into undulating waves of silver and black. The car bounced in the rocky roadway. Its lights were off, and the driver navigated by moonlight. The chill wind turned Flinders's collar into a necklace of ice. He thought he heard gunfire echoing in the expanse.

Silent villages flowed past. Crooked streets lined with dark buildings crisscrossed in front of the windscreen. Flinders could see the lights of Baghdad twinkling across the distant horizon. A heavy smell of burnt wood surrounded the passengers. Jagged black and gray shapes loomed out of a smoky mist. White shapes sprawled across the roadway. The swollen body of a dead horse, its stiff legs extended, forced the driver to swerve. A black bird pecked at the carcass.

The car crept through the village.

"This village has been burnt." Flinders leaned out and stared at the shapes. "Those are bodies."

"Ashuri," the driver said.

The car turned a corner and abruptly stopped before a lone woman. She knelt in the street in front of the car. Light from the moon outlined her bent figure. Her hair hung disheveled over her long dress. Small bodies surrounded her. Empty clothes littered the street. Flinders heard her mournful wail. The sad sound echoed off the ruins around her.

Gazelda covered her eyes. "Those are her children."

Pettigrew put his hands on the sides of his face. "She must have been there all night."

Flinders touched the driver's shoulder. "Please wait." He got out and went to the woman. "Come with us, please," he told her.

She did not move. Cold moonlight reflected off the tears on her cheeks.

"Driver, speak to her in Arabic."

The driver shook his head. "No Arabic."

"What do you mean?"

"Ashuri only. All Ashuri. All dead. Kurds kill."

"Then speak to her in Assyrian."

"Cannot."

"She will die here."

"Yes."

Flinders pleaded again. "Please come with us."

"No leave her children," the driver said and again shook his head.

Flinders could hear Gazelda crying in the car. Pettigrew pushed himself through the open car door. "Flinders . . ."

"Stay back." Flinders waved him away.

The woman remained motionless; she stared unblinking at the bodies. A chance breeze ruffled the clothes of the small shapes.

Flinders knelt beside her. "Please, you must come with us."

She moaned but did not move.

"Please. We can help," Flinders whispered in her ear.

She looked at him; her eyes were pools of despair.

The driver cut in. "Husband dead, children dead, no want to live."

Scudding clouds cut the moonlight into long strands. Bars of white light streamed across the still figure.

Flinders rose and opened the car door. The door squeaked and then thudded shut.

"Drive on," he said quietly. "There is nothing we can do."

As the car passed her, the woman's eyes stared into Flinders's, asking him what she did to deserve this.

"Nothing," he mouthed. "You did nothing." Then time shifted for him.

The Christian woman looked down from her cross. "We did nothing either. We wished to sing and pray and tend our flocks."

"I know. So did the Assyrians whose bodies lie here."

What will you do here? he asked himself.

But there was nothing he could do. He could save a baby bird. But he could not save a woman who had lost her children.

Flinders turned and looked back. A still figure was outlined by pale light; it dwindled as the car drove away.

The desert was silent for the rest of the journey. Flinders dozed and then startled awake. A woman's eyes stared at him. Small bodies rose up and circled him, their faces white with death. They cried and reached for him. He woke up in a sweat. The car was moving slowly between large eucalyptus trees. Their smell filled the air, and moonlight threaded between their twisted trunks. He fell back asleep, but the dream kept coming back.

The pungent smell of eucalyptus flooded his sleeping senses.

The call to prayer echoed over the city. Mist shrouded its domes and minarets. Fingers of sunlight crept between shadowy spires. Overhanging porches shrank the morning sky to a thin ribbon of blue. The car drove down the uneven cobbles and pulled to a stop; its engine clunked off. Flinders got out, rubbed his eyes, and looked down the narrow street. "It has been a long night." *A long and terrible night.*

Pettigrew followed and stared around like an owl emerging from a tree.

"The home of the Abbasids, Thomas. This is where Scheherazade began. Look sharp—she may cross the street in front of you."

Flinders's eyes traveled into the distance. *This is an ancient street. What has it seen in a thousand years? Did Harun al-Rashid parade down this street with a massive bodyguard dressed in the black of the Abbasids? Did the drums rattle and the horses clop? Did Aladdin skip down these cobbles clutching his lamp?*

Flinders looked at Gazelda still in the back seat. "Come along, Miss Jones, don't just sit there." She tumbled out. "You still look a little green from the sea voyage." He tried out an evil smile and gave her a quick wink. "Perhaps we should have taken the longer route by land."

He closed the car door and peered at the crumbling wall with its spike-studded wooden doorway.

"Well, British Intelligence has certainly concealed itself this time. This looks like something out of the seventeenth century." He laughed. "Shall we knock or blow trumpets?" He banged on the door. The heavy wood quivered; its iron hinges rattled. "This appears to be an old Mamluk fortress—just the thing for a lively Intelligence crew."

An unseen bar on the other side of the door grated as it was withdrawn.

The door opened, and an unformed guard surveyed them. "Please come in. Miss Bell is expecting you." The guard led them across a tree-lined courtyard and opened another door—a door also studded with iron spikes. Turrets with archers' slits overhung the trees. *This reminds me of the Krak des Chevaliers.* They went in. A long hall unrolled before them. Rows of doors with glass panels slid by; typewriters clicked behind them. Bare wood squeaked under their boots. The hall smelled of tobacco and old paper. The guard knocked at a small door. The sign on its dusty glass read EMPLOYEES ONLY.

"Come."

Gertrude stood up from behind a desk, her green eyes fixed on Pettigrew. "Ah, Thomas, you are back," she said casually, as if they had just departed yesterday. "And Flinders, how good to see you again." She waved them in but remained standing behind her desk. "But who is this?"

"Miss Jones. Father Divinius sent her along." Flinders gave her a playful scowl.

"I see. Do sit down. I have ordered tea." Flinders watched her green eyes as they searched Pettigrew's face. "It has been a long time."

"Yes, it has."

They sat in small wooden chairs that were neatly arranged in front of the desk.

"You did not say goodbye when you left Istanbul."

"There was no time."

"You did not write," she said. Her green eyes accused Pettigrew. *They see only him.*

"I did not know where you were."

"You look well."

"You look well also, Gertrude," Pettigrew said, his voice soft this time.

An orderly wheeled in a tea cart. Its shelves were crammed with dishes of sandwiches and pots of tea and coffee covered to keep warm. Cups and saucers were stacked to one side. The orderly pulled out several small folding tables and set them up.

Everything is tidy here.

"I am well, thank you." Gertrude stood up and came around to the front of her desk.

"Tea, Miss Jones? Flinders?" She poured the tea, setting cups in front of both. "Milk, Thomas?"

"No, thank you."

"A biscuit, perhaps." She handed him a cup. The saucer trembled slightly as their hands met under it.

"Yes, thank you." Pettigrew took a sip and then put his cup down. "You have not changed."

"No, have you?"

"No."

Gertrude returned to the desk.

The three sat in the stiff wooden chairs.

Neither had changed. Flinders sighed heavily. They were painful to watch.

The office was cramped; folders and papers were neatly arranged in shelves that ran along the walls. A small prayer rug lay in front of the desk. Flinders looked around. A plain oak desk sat in front of him. The desktop was bare except for a small rectangle of glass that served as a blotter. *The uncluttered desk of an uncluttered mind.* Large vases of tulips with twisted stems resting on plant stands stood on either side. Gertrude leaned forward in her chair. The glass blotter reflected the fire in her hair.

"Did you miss me?" Her eyes were intent, her lips pursed.

"Yes."

She frowned gently. "Whatever happened to that Badawi woman?"

"I do not know."

"Oh."

Flinders glanced at Gazelda; her eyes were wide. "They are old friends."

"I see."

Flinders put down his cup. "Gertrude, we are here about Saint Thomas," he said. "We think that the Veiled One has stolen his bones." He unfolded the file that Father Divinius had given him and placed it on the small table between them. "The relics were stolen from the basilica in Erbil. We think that they may have been transported to Baghdad." He peered at the brown folder. "There is a suggestion that the relics may still be in the al-Attabiyah district." He glanced at Gazelda.

She smiled.

Gertrude lit a cigarette. "You two have caused quite a stir. After you left, the Veiled One had all the harem guards killed." She put the cigarette down and leaned over the desk. "Some of the guards were impaled on their own scimitars. Others were drenched in raki and set on fire." She frowned. "The Veiled One is ruthless."

"We know." Pettigrew rubbed his shoulder.

Gertrude stood up, leaned over the tea cart, and looked at Gazelda. "More tea?"

"Yes, with a little cream, thank you."

"Another biscuit for you, Flinders?"

"Yes, thank you."

She returned to the desk and sat back.

"Thomas, you have taken his mother's most prized possession, and you have killed his trusted lieutenant. You have created a mortal enemy, and now you want to challenge him again?" She looked hard at Pettigrew. "Are you so willing to risk death?"

Pettigrew looked at Flinders. Flinders nodded.

"Yes," Pettigrew said.

"So be it for you two, but what about her?" Gertrude gestured at Gazelda.

"I can answer for myself," Gazelda straightened in her chair. "The answer is 'yes.'"

Flinders arched an eyebrow and then nodded in grudging approval.

Gertrude waved the orderly out. When the door closed behind him, she spoke. "You have come at a dangerous time. The Ottoman government is in a state of collapse. There are local warlords running all over the place."

"Gertrude, we passed a procession of women and men in Basrah." Flinders leaned forward in his seat. "The driver said they were going to be executed."

"Armenians?"

"The driver said they were 'Armini.'"

"In Basrah?" Gertrude frowned. "I did not think the executions went so far south."

"Then we drove through a burned-out village just south of here." Flinders looked at her intently. "There were bodies everywhere and a woman sitting among her dead children."

"An Assyrian village?'

"I believe so."

"A few Assyrian villages have been burned outside of Baghdad." Gertrude rubbed her eyes. She looked tired.

"Most of the violence is farther north of Baghdad. Both government and independent warlords are involved. It is a mix of regular troops, Cossack irregulars, and Kurdish tribesmen."

"These would include the Veiled One?"

"Indeed so. He may be orchestrating some of the violence."

Flinders sat back in his chair. "The firman that the Assyrians found was made in Baghdad."

"Ah, I'm glad that you reminded me." Gertrude smiled. "Divinius cabled me a description of the firman. I gave it to the staff weaving expert to see what he could find."

"You have a staff weaving expert?"

"Of course. We are a full-service intelligence agency."

She unfolded a paper. "The expert confirmed that the firman was made in Baghdad. He said that it was probably woven by a small shop in the old section of the city. The shop has been there for years. He inquired about it, but his sources said that there hadn't been any activity there for many days."

"Do you have an address?" Flinders asked. "We would like to investigate it anyway."

"Yes, it's the last shop on the left, just before the mosque. It's in a small cul-de-sac."

"We will go tomorrow."

"You will have to be very, very careful. This is a dangerous time."

"We will go in disguise."

"You don't fully understand." Gertrude's green eyes fixed on him. "There are competing factions attempting to gain control of the country. They are ruthless, and they blame Christians for destroying the empire." She lit a cigarette. "They want to 'Turkify' the old empire. Every ethnic group that is not pure Turkish must be destroyed."

"We have seen some of that."

"Remember the old general who gave you the address of the Veiled One's villa?" Gertrude leaned forward in her chair and rested her elbows on the desk. "He was originally allied with the Veiled One. Then he switched sides and betrayed him. The Veiled One's revenge was merciless."

"He seemed very nervous when we talked to him."

"He was right to be nervous," Gertrude said. "The Veiled One's men raided his villa on the Black Sea. Our agent—a young boy that we furnished to the general—was there. He hid in a closet and then escaped. He said the shouting and screaming was terrible. The Veiled One's men killed everyone. Men, women, and children. The floors ran red with blood."

She blew a smoke ring.

"Go on, please," Flinders said. "Then what happened?"

"They dragged the general to the beach. They buried him in the sand. Only his head was visible. They formed a circle around him and laughed as the tide began to creep on the beach. He screamed and gurgled as the water swept over him. And then he was silent."

"What happened to the boy?"

"He is safe. Kudret has taken all his agents to Mosul. They are hidden in a monastery near Mosul. But we expect they will have to be moved to Baghdad."

"Kudret is here?" Pettigrew joined in.

"Yes, he fled Istanbul after the sultan was overthrown. His koceks went into hiding—the new ruling factions considered them symbols of the depraved empire. Some of them were tortured and killed."

"And Mariam." Flinders's face tensed. "What about Mariam?"

Gertrude blew another smoke ring. "Mariam left Istanbul years ago. She went back to her village in Urmia. She has a husband and two small children."

Flinders nodded. "So she is safe?"

"I do not know," Gertrude said. "We have reports that Assyrian villages in Urmia have been attacked by marauding Kurdish irregulars."

"Oh."

Gazelda searched Flinders's face from behind her large spectacles. Her eyes were round with concern.

Gertrude was silent for a moment. "Mariam," she said, "tried to teach you to belly dance."

"I know."

"You were not very good." Gertrude's eyes twinkled and then became wistful. "Mariam . . . yes, I saw the way your face looked when you watched her at the embassy."

Gazelda sighed.

Gertrude sighed as well, looked at Pettigrew, and whispered to herself, "I wish a man would look at me like that."

The room became quiet. Echoes of smoke rings floated above Gertrude's desk. The click of typewriters carried in from behind the glass door. An orderly knocked, entered, and handed Gertrude a sheaf of papers. She read them and frowned in concentration. The ceiling fan hummed overhead, its blades slowly beating the air.

"I'll take care of it."

The orderly disappeared.

Finally, she looked up. "After you recovered the statue of Aphrodite, the Veiled One became more vicious and more brutal. He swore to take vengeance on anyone who had any connection with his mother's death. He started to kill Ottoman officers. One of the officers he killed was the only son of a general who now heads the ruling coalition. Their troops fought in the north."

"Aphrodite has always had a bloody history," Flinders said. *What is it about these ancient religious figures that brings so much suffering?* And his time in the desert had only intensified that sense of suffering.

"The Veiled One's army was defeated; the slaughter was terrible." Gertrude shook her head. "Bodies were everywhere." She scanned the file. "There are photographs."

"And the Veiled One?" Flinders asked.

"He escaped. We think he is in Baghdad."

"And Saint Thomas's relics?"

"They are probably with him."

"So how do we find him?"

"A dragoman."

"A dragoman?" Flinders was puzzled. "Divinius said something about dragomen."

"You'll see." Getrude smiled. "We are quite efficient. Now go and find a hotel. I recommend the Khan. It's been around since the sixteenth century."

"The sixteenth century?" Flinders balked.

"Don't worry—it has been modernized." Gertrude winked at

Gazelda. "I'm sure that it will be more than suitable for a person of your elegance."

Gazelda hid a smile behind her hands.

They got up and left. Gertrude waved a cheery goodbye, but her eyes never left Pettigrew.

The door clicked behind them. Typewriters chattered as they walked down the hall. A guard waved them out. The car with the blue headlights was waiting. The sun began to set behind the ancient minarets; its ochre outlined their spires. Flinders looked at the skyline.

Yes, Scheherazade would have seen this many centuries ago.

But what would she think now?

☙

The drive to the Khan Hotel was short.

The car stopped in front of two enormous glass doors. A kaftaned doorman waved them in. The lobby glittered with crystal chandeliers. A statue of Isis faced them from her pedestal. Laughter floated out from a glittering bar. *The atmosphere is quite different here. I don't see any guards or sinister men in black suits.* The deskman smiled a hello. Flinders's ears caught the sound of soft music. "Roses from the South," he said, recognizing it. "I think we shall enjoy our stay here. Come along, Miss Jones—let us find our rooms."

Flinders headed toward a grand staircase flanked by potted palms. "Dragomen, indeed."

He listened to the waltz and thought, *It is a soft melody from another time.* "I was in Vienna once on a case," Flinders said softly. "There was a park, and in that park, there was a statue of Strauss playing his violin. This very waltz music we are hearing now . . . it comes into my mind now." *The statue was old, some of it covered in gold, and the music soared in my mind. It soars here as well, but here, its softness conceals a terrible reality.*

The hallway gleamed gold and red as they walked. Pettigrew turned his key and said good night. Flinders and Gazelda stopped in front of her room.

"We have an address," she said, "and we must be up early tomorrow."

"Good night, Miss Jones."

The door clicked closed.

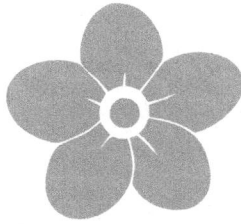

FOUR

Che Gelida Manina

Flinders, sitting behind his newspaper, watched as Pettigrew surveyed the lobby. "An idyllic scene," he heard Pettigrew say, "but we are missing someone." Flinders smiled and rattled the newspaper pages. Pettigrew looked around but appeared not to notice him. Flinders coughed and blew a smoke ring. Pettigrew did not glance in his direction. Flinders put the paper down and called loudly for the waiter. Pettigrew turned to speak with Gazelda.

Morning sunlight played through the hotel's tall windows and warmed Flinders's back. Two older women played cards at a low table. A man in a gray suit and red fez sat on a sofa and read a travel brochure. The desk clerks lounged in their seats. A cat curled up in one of the chairs, its tail waving languidly in the warm sun. Flinders followed Pettigrew's eyes as they swept the room. "All he sees is an old priest smoking a cigarette and opening a newspaper in a corner." *All those contests with Holmes have proven their worth.* The priest stuffed out his cigarette. *Yes indeed, they were most worthwhile.*

Traffic noise filtered in from the street.

"Where is Flinders?" Gazelda looked at Pettigrew. Flinders suppressed a smile, though he knew they wouldn't see it from behind his beard.

"He is always late." Pettigrew grumbled. "He would be late to his own funeral."

"Flinders is not late." The priest put the paper down, stood up, and walked directly in front of them. "He has been waiting for you two for almost an hour."

"We didn't recognize you," Gazelda said in startled surprise.

"Of course not—that is the idea."

"How did you manage that disguise?"

"Practice, Miss Jones, practice."

"Now, let me look at you." Flinders eyed both of them. Pettigrew wore a long gray cassock with a high hat. Gazelda was dressed in a gray robe with a shawl. "Yes, they did a good job outfitting you in London. Divinius was right."

Gazelda smiled. "You look so authentic."

"Certainly." His beard waggled as he spoke. "My disguises are always authentic. Did I tell you about the time Holmes and I had a 'face-off' challenge?" He fluffed his beard. "We dressed as parish priests and had Father Brown be the judge." He looked at Pettigrew. "You remember Father Brown, don't you? He wrote you a letter asking your advice on becoming a detective."

Pettigrew nodded; his gold chains rattled.

Flinders lifted a hand. "Do not rattle your chains. Priests do not rattle chains."

Pettigrew frowned.

"To continue, Miss Jones," Flinders said, "we went to a local pub. We looked very ecumenical. There was a brawl. You know how

Londoners get when they're in their cups." Flinders laughed. "We entered, Father Brown blessed everybody, and the place quieted down at once."

"Who won?" Gazelda asked.

"Never mind that."

"I like your eyebrows." Gazelda grinned.

"Thank you—eyebrows are quite difficult. Even Holmes had trouble with them. I once wrote a short monograph on eyebrows."

"I should like to read it."

Flinders frowned. "Let me look again. Yes, there is need for improvement." He reached into his cassock and discreetly pulled out another beard and then looked around to make sure no one was watching before handing it to Pettigrew. "Thomas, put this on. The little wires go over your ears. No, Thomas—don't just play with your beard in the middle of a hotel lobby. Go off to a corner. Ah, that's better." Flinders peered at him. "Now let me see you walk."

Pettigrew took a few steps.

"No, you need a slight limp."

"A slight limp?"

"Character, you know," Flinders said. "Just imagine that you got hurt in a monastery soccer game."

"Soccer? What are you talking about?"

"Priests do play soccer, you know." Flinders's beard twitched, tickling his face. "You are supposed to be an old priest, so limp. Thomas, sometimes I despair. I knew I should have made you take acting lessons."

He turned to Gazelda. "Now you—stop grinning. You're supposed to be an acolyte. Acolytes are serious; they think of divine things." He thought a moment. "Imagine you just stubbed your toe—that will give you the right expression."

Gazelda grimaced.

"No, no, no, a thousand times, no. Do not look like you have just eaten a persimmon—act as though you are in spiritual rapture. Rapture, understand? Rapture."

Flinders shook his head. "Now I understand why stage directors get gray hair. And take off those glasses."

"But I won't be able to see."

"Wonderful." He clapped his hands. "Then you will have to walk slowly, as though you were meditating." He took a deep breath. "Now, we will take a car to the outskirts of the street where the weaver has their shop and then walk in. Gertrude has arranged for a man with a donkey to meet us."

"Donkey?" Pettigrew's eyes widened. "What do you mean, a *donkey*?"

"Of course, a donkey. I will walk and lead the donkey." He smiled. "What could be more disarming than an old priest leading a donkey?"

"Flinders, you can't bring a donkey to a field investigation."

"You have no imagination."

"Suppose there's shooting?"

"The donkey will run away of its own accord."

"Suppose we have to flee?"

"We will just put Miss Jones on the donkey, and she will gallop off. We can run after her. You *can* ride, can't you?"

Gazelda looked concerned. "No."

He clucked. "Sometimes, I despair."

Pettigrew shook his head. "Flinders, no donkey."

"You are a toad," Flinders said. He pushed them out the door and toward a waiting car.

"And Thomas, straighten your hat."

❧

The car ground to a stop with a cloud of dirty gray exhaust. The donkey rolled a white eye at it. They got out; the car doors slammed shut. Flinders spoke to the man holding the donkey and handed him a few coins for his trouble. Flinders scratched the donkey's ear and then headed toward the cobbled street, leaving the man and his gentle beast staring after him. "Her name is Aminah, the man said—Aminah means 'trusted one.' I miss her already." He looked sadly at Pettigrew. "She was quite friendly. If you had petted her, you would feel differently." He took one last backward glance. The man was already lost in the crowd as he led the donkey away.

"Ah, the last swish of a playful tail."

"Flinders, we haven't gone fifty paces."

"I know, but where is the gentle pull on the lead?" Flinders bowed his head. "Where *is* the soft sound of hooves on the cobbles?"

"The soft sound of hooves on the cobbles?"

"Possibly a wistful bray."

Pettigrew's jaw dropped. "A wistful bray?"

"Thomas, you have no heart."

"We are detectives," Pettigrew growled, "not animal trainers."

Flinders grinned. "Donkeys are man's best friend."

"I think that you have got that slightly wrong."

"Well then, we must soldier on." Flinders pushed them toward the street. "Slower, Miss Jones, slower. Try to look devout." He grimaced. "No, no, no. How many times must I say it? Not sick to your stomach—think of Joan of Arc. Sarah Bernhardt, where are you when I need you?" Flinders rolled his eyes. "*Holmes* could do a better acolyte."

They walked into the waiting street. Its noise and clamor grew louder as they approached. The street of the silk weavers was narrow and crooked. A sliver of sky trickled between dark awnings. Its entrance was flanked by large wooden gates, studded with iron spikes.

Gazelda pointed at the spikes. "During the time of the Abbasids, every community had walls and gates. Everyone was armed, and the wealthy hired armed retainers."

"So now you are an Arabist?" Flinders adjusted his tall hat. "Where did you learn that?"

"I read *The Arabian Nights*."

"Really, which version?" Flinders fluffed his beard.

"The Burton edition."

"You mean the one with all the erotic endnotes?"

"Yes."

"The one that was declared unfit for a gentle person's library?"

"Yes, that one."

"And did you find it interesting?" Flinders smoothed his cassock.

Gazelda managed a shy smile. "Indeed, so."

"Your husband should have forbidden it."

"I have no husband. I do as I please."

"So you do." Flinders straightened his gold chains. "So you do. Thomas, have you brought your gun?"

"It is in my waistband."

"Good. You take the right side, and I will watch the left." Flinders frowned. "I sense that we are being watched. Gertrude's security may not be as tight as she thinks. Someone has discovered that we're coming here."

He stopped at a brass-maker's booth and peered into a polished brass tray. "A good mirror." He squinted. "I can see him behind us. He is wearing a gray robe and a striped kufiyah."

Pettigrew took out a gold watch the size of a small saucer and held it up as though he was telling the time. Then he studied its polished case. "I'll keep him in sight. He's pretending to buy some fruit." Flinders watched as Pettigrew studied the watch. "He's too obvious—there must be someone else we cannot see."

"I don't see anyone, but I think you're right."

Flinders dodged a boy selling flowers. "Don't get separated by the crowd," he said.

"Watch yourself." He caught Gazelda's hand as she stumbled over a fallen melon. "Stumbling is not helpful."

"I'm not wearing my glasses, remember?"

"Nevertheless, acolytes do not stumble."

"I've lost him," Pettigrew said. "He disappeared behind a stack of bread loaves."

Flinders brushed aside a stray awning. "The light keeps changing in here."

A line of carts rumbled by them. Weavers and fruit sellers called out their wares. Animals of all kinds laden with goods passed by.

The donkey would have been a perfect cover.

"Wait, there he is," Flinders hissed. "This one is in black. Keep moving, Miss Jones. We are coming to the end of the street."

"Gertrude said that it was the last shop on the right, just before the mosque," Pettigrew said. "Well, there is the mosque, and I can see the Tigris behind it."

Bales of wool blocked their way. Flinders saw a small alley, half-hidden by awnings. "Looks deserted."

The alley ended in a small cul-de-sac. Mounds of dirty straw and garbage littered its cobbles.

Flinders sniffed. "This is vintage garbage. I haven't smelled anything like this since the City of the Dead."

Gazelda smiled. "Yes, it is a good garbage, but not a great garbage."

Flinders chuckled. "You have become a sommelier of garbage?"

"Your nose is too tender." Pettigrew smiled. "As I said before, you should smell an operating room."

"I think this may be the shop." Gazelda pointed to a low doorway. There was no awning, and no table of goods. Stray pieces of carpet littered the ground. A rat scurried across the door frame.

Flinders sniffed the air. "There is a strange smell. And lots of flies." He tried the wooden door. "Thomas, lend me a hand. Gazelda, please keep watch." They pried the door open; part of the old frame splintered. Rats squeaked and scuttled away.

"Whew, that is terrible." Gazelda held her nose.

"Decomposition," Pettigrew said. "There's a dead body inside. It wouldn't take long in this heat."

They crossed the low threshold and went in. The room was dark; beams of sunlight filtered through small holes in the wooden walls. Dust rose when they took a step. Furniture and carpets lay jumbled about the floor. Several white shapes lay tangled in the debris.

Flinders stepped over a dead rat. "Nothing moves here. I don't like the feel of this place."

"Flinders, come over here," Pettigrew beckoned. "Look."

Flinders saw a small body lying in front of a loom. The loom was broken, pieces of wood and carpet were scattered about, and the body lay twisted in front of it. Its head was twisted at an odd angle, and strands of gray hair covered the face. "It's her," Flinders said, "the woman who wove the firman."

"How do you know?" Pettigrew asked.

"She's older, and she's small—less than seven stone—and she wears a bracelet on her right arm." Flinders pointed to the loom. "See that fabric? It's the same weave—she was weaving another firman when she died."

Gazelda bent close and picked up a loom shuttle. "I think you are right." She held it up to the dim light. "The weave has the same unusual pattern."

He sniffed. "And there is another scent besides decomposition—hashish, I think. Miss Jones, could you give us the benefit of your intimate acquaintance with hashish?"

Gazelda screwed up her face and sniffed. "Baghdad Gold. The assailant is probably local."

"And can you tell anything else about him?"

"Yes, he was a short man, probably around eight stone in weight, and right-handed."

"And how did you deduce that?"

"I looked at the woman's wound. It was shallow to the right of her neck and deeper toward the left. Since she faced her assailant, the knife went from right to left. She was slain by someone using his right arm."

"Very good. Anything else?"

"The wound slanted slightly down to the left of her neck. The assailant was about the same height as the woman. If he had been taller, the wound would have slanted up."

"And his age?"

"I cannot tell."

"But I can," Flinders said, pointing at the dead woman's fist. "She had a hair strand clutched in her hand. I saw it at once. The woman's hair is gray, but the hair in her hand is shiny black—a young person's hair. The assailant was a young man, perhaps in his late twenties."

Flinders smiled. "I once wrote a short monograph on hair follicles."

"I read it." Gazelda grinned. "Your discussion of the link between early baldness and murder was most impressive."

Flinders bowed slightly. "I am honored."

"There is more." Pettigrew looked up at them. "Her stomach is swollen—she's been dead for at least two days." He examined the body. "Her neck has been broken, and there are bruises on her face. I think she was tortured." He felt around. "Yes, a rib has been broken." Pettigrew stood up and stepped over some overturned furniture. "This place is destroyed; someone was searching it."

"But for what?"

"The search was done at night." Flinders hunted around. "During the day, the room would have been bright with sunlight through the open door. But at night, it would be hard to see. And look, the oil lamps have been turned over. They have smoke smudges, which means they were lit when the attack occurred. I'm surprised that this place didn't catch fire." Flinders walked carefully about the room. "I should have brought my magnifying glass."

"You mean *my* magnifying glass."

"Details."

"Some areas are untouched; others are torn apart." Pettigrew looked about the room. "Whoever did this was in a great hurry and didn't do a thorough search."

"Quite right, Thomas."

"There might have been screaming."

"Exactly, Miss Jones."

Pettigrew knelt by one white shape. "An old man . . . his hands are cut. He was trying to defend himself." Pettigrew pulled aside a blood-stained kufiyah that covered the face. "His throat has been slit." He looked up. "Just like old George in the Museum."

"Hashshashin?" Flinders looked at Pettigrew.

"Most probably."

Flinders turned and stepped across the ruins of the carpet weaver's pitiful remains.

"Wait a minute." He bent over a body. "Look at this—another old man. The rats have been gnawing on his body." He knelt. "There is something in his hand. There is a great deal of blood. It's streaked, as though he was trying to crawl as he bled to death. He must have been reaching for it." He carefully pried open the stiff fingers. "It's a paper with Arabic writing. Whoever did this must have thought he was dead and left. But he wasn't quite dead."

"Gertrude could probably translate it."

"Indeed."

"It's time to go." Flinders pushed them toward the door. "I have seen two shadows move across the wall. Someone is watching us." He put the paper under his cassock. "Mind you don't slip on any blood, Miss Jones."

"It's dried."

"Of course it is—these people have been dead for several days."

Flinders cautiously poked his head out the door and brushed the flies away. "The street is empty in front of us. I don't see anybody." The sunlight was blinding as they left the building. "Now, Miss Jones, let's hear your Greek," Flinders whispered. "Say goodbye in a loud voice and thank them for weaving a beautiful surplice."

"But they are dead!"

"Humor me."

Pettigrew whispered, "I think there is a third. They are planning something."

"Well, if so, they're probably going to use knives." Flinders squinted in the brightness. "Hashshashin don't use guns. . . . At least, I assume that's who they are. As long as we keep track of them, we will be fine."

Gazelda was not convinced. "Suppose you're wrong?" she said.

"Well, then, things will get very exciting."

Flinders strolled calmly into the cul-de-sac. "We must act as though nothing has happened. Whoever is watching us will be confused," he muttered to himself. "Holmes was a master at this kind of deception. He knew how to appear nonchalant in tense situations, and so must we." He turned his face to Gazelda, whose expression was stiff. "Smile and be delightful, Miss Jones."

Gazelda looked pained. She held her hands together in front of her.

"And please do not stumble. Stumbling is not helpful." Flinders grinned. "I think I said that before. Perhaps you didn't hear."

"*Delightful?*" Gazelda said in a low voice. "How can I be delightful when there are killers lurking about?"

"You have much to learn, Miss Jones. Now, keep walking."

"How can she keep walking when you made her take off her glasses?" asked Pettigrew.

"I can see why you never became a stage director, Thomas." Flinders rubbed his nose. "Ah, the Savoy—I miss the music and the lyrics."

"The Savoy, indeed," Pettigrew said, peering into a side street.

"Do you like Gilbert and Sullivan, Miss Jones?"

Gazelda's laughter burbled up.

"I'll take that as a no."

Flinders searched his surroundings. "Thomas, did I ever tell you that I tried out for the part of Major General Stanley?" Flinders rolled his eyes to his left, where a slight movement behind some barrels caught his attention. "I think he is over there."

"I would have thought the Pirate King to be more to your liking." Pettigrew shaded his eyes. "You are right, and there may be a fourth."

"I saw him. He is behind the fruit stand."

"I'll take the two in front. You shoot the two behind."

"In the meantime, let us proceed." Flinders turned into the crooked street. "Ah, the exoticism of *The Arabian Nights*. Come, Miss Jones— think of the beautiful Jauhara, the Sea King's daughter."

"The Sea King's daughter?"

"Perhaps you missed that part in your hurry to get to the end-notes. Thomas, what are we to do with today's illiterate youth?" Flinders waved them on. "So far, so good. I can only see three so far. We're still ahead of them. And, Thomas, don't forget to limp." He frowned through his beard. "You can't limp in and then come dancing out."

Pettigrew laughed. "I shall try to be more convincing."

"This wasn't a chiropodist establishment, you know."

"Nonsense, my back feels better already."

"Thomas, your back may be fine, but your beard is a disaster. Please, straighten it."

"You are too picky."

Gazelda muttered to herself, "Who are these men? I think you two would argue in the face of death itself."

Inji once said something like that.

"Argue? *Argue?*" Flinders shook his head. "I *knew* I should have brought that donkey along."

"What is this about a donkey?"

"I told you once—they are man's best friend."

"You said that before," Pettigrew grumbled. "You are repeating yourself in your dotage."

"Anyway, as the king once said, 'March away.'"

"This is Baghdad, not Harfleur," Pettigrew said.

"You are illiterate."

"Your eyebrow is drooping."

Flinders sighed. "No one is perfect."

"I think the fourth one is behind those bales."

"Let me look." Flinders paused to inspect some brass dallahs. "Beautifully inscribed. These are art objects disguised as coffee pots. And polished to perfection. You are correct, sir, he is behind the bales."

"I will cover him," Pettigrew said.

"I have the other three in my sights."

"Well done."

"Could you move a little faster?" Flinders whispered.

"I am trying to be cat-like," Pettigrew said, dodging a cart. "But it is difficult to imitate a limping cat."

"Think of Dick Whittington's cat."

"Dick Whittington's cat did not limp."

"A cat may look at a king, but your cat has mumps."

"A cat cannot have mumps," Pettigrew huffed.

"I just call them the way I see them." Flinders pushed Gazelda ahead of him.

"Now you have become an umpire at a cricket match? I think there is another," Pettigrew whispered.

"I see him," said Flinders. "Cover me, please."

"Consider it done."

"Your cat moves like a wounded duck."

"At least my duck has matching eyebrows," Pettigrew grumbled.

"You are a toad."

"A toad, sir?" Pettigrew slid his hand under his cassock and fingered his pistol. "You've said that before."

"Yes, a toad." Flinders loosened his sash. "A toad from Toad Hall."

"You've been at the children's books again."

"Excellent reading." Flinders crossed the narrow street. "Much better than your musty medical journals."

Flinders drew his pistol. "As the Red Queen said, 'We must begin at the beginning.'"

"The Red Queen didn't say that," Pettigrew said, stepping around a large stack of fruit. "But you do remind me of the Mad Hatter."

"Better than the March Hare." Flinders sighted his pistol. "As the Spanish say, 'the moment of truth' is at hand."

"Not quite." Pettigrew peered back at the alley. "Ah, I think we have cleared them."

Flinders squinted. "Indeed so. Come along, Miss Jones." He grinned. "The Cheshire cat awaits."

Gazelda shook her head. "Children's books."

They walked slowly back down the street of the weavers. For Flinders, the last few steps were surreal. The street seemed to have grown longer and more crowded than before; vendors' faces were frozen into grotesque grins. Carts appeared from nowhere and threatened to hit them. Horses and donkeys laid their ears back as they passed. Fruits and vegetables rolled in their path; awnings swayed and flapped in their faces. Small boys darted and made obscene gestures. Hawkers cried out to them as they passed.

Flinders smiled and nodded. Pettigrew managed several gentle waves and pulled at his beard. "Be careful with that, Thomas—we can't have your beard falling into the street."

Gazelda looked pained.

"That is wonderful, Miss Jones." Flinders smiled from behind his beard. "I told you that imagining your stubbed toe would do it. And I think that I will dawdle at this fruit stand while you two go on ahead through the gates."

"More aplomb?" Gazelda frowned.

"No, he is just giving us time to get out of here," Pettigrew whispered. "Whoever is watching will have to wait behind him."

Flinders waited, perusing the fruit, and caught up with them when they were not far from the automobile.

They passed through the gates, reached the car, and got in. The driver smiled.

Gazelda whispered to Pettigrew, "The man has ice in his veins."

"You noticed." Pettigrew grinned. "We are professionals, you know."

"Why do you babble like that?"

"It relieves the tension. Surgeons in operating rooms babble as well."

"Relieves the tension?"

"Yes, we must be relaxed."

"Are you always relaxed?"

"We try to be. That's why we are still alive."

"I see," Gazelda said.

Once they were inside, Flinders stretched back in the seat. "Tamarinds, anybody?"

"No?" Pettigrew said tentatively.

"All right, I will try one." Gazelda took a fruit.

Flinders peeled a large tamarind. "Perhaps Gertrude can have someone whip up a nice glass of tamarind juice. It is said to be excellent for the dusty throat. Now, Miss Jones, you can put your glasses back on."

"Thank you, sir."

Flinders smiled. "I must say that I am impressed."

Gazelda smiled.

"Yes, very impressed indeed." Flinders carefully removed his tall hat. "Miss Jones, you were devout beyond belief."

"I imagined myself to be in the presence of ancient icons."

"And Thomas, you had the limp of a man who has given a thousand sermons."

"Yes, and all of them uplifting."

"Another tamarind?" Flinders asked them.

Pettigrew shook his head. "I think not. It's too close to dinner."

"I may have missed my calling," Flinders said, unbuttoning his cassock. "I believe that I will speak to Father Brown on our return."

Pettigrew unhooked his false beard. "The thought of you blessing people boggles my mind."

"You've been boggled a great deal lately. Perhaps a tincture of holy water would help."

Gazelda covered a grin with her hand.

"Now for the hotel, and a bath," Pettigrew said.

The car started with a roar of exhaust. Flinders turned in his seat and looked back at the gates. *I am slowing down. I wonder if I could have stopped them if they had attacked.* He shook his head. *I wonder.*

Pettigrew knocked and came in.

"I'm almost done." Flinders closed a cufflink. "Thomas, a pressed shirt is like a breath of heaven." He slipped on a dark coat and smoothed its lapels. "Yes, a nice shoulder line. Now I am ready for dinner." He twisted back and forth to see himself better in the mirror. "Thomas, we live in an age of slovenliness. What did the bard say? 'Nothing so becomes a man . . .'"

"I think King Henry was talking about humility, not about dress shirts." Pettigrew tightened his tie. "You may have had a chance encounter with humility, but I doubt it."

"Humility has nothing to do with it." Flinders flicked an imaginary thread off his sleeve. "A man must be elegant in dress, decisive in action, and sensitive to the needs of others."

"You sound like a medieval knight."

"Indeed, it is an ancient creed."

"I had no idea." Pettigrew folded a collar. "All this time, I thought you were just an ordinary detective."

Flinders adjusted his lapels.

"Flinders, you are hopelessly out of date. Nobody believes that nonsense these days."

"I do, and that is enough. Besides, we are all medieval knights: Thomas, Lawrence, Gertrude, Kudret, and even Gazelda. We strive like knights on a flaming chess board. A chess board whose play is without end. And who says that a knight must wear steel armor? Any kind of dress is enough; even a dress shirt is sufficient." Flinders inspected a cuff link. "You don't have to clank around."

Pettigrew straightened his tie.

Flinders turned and stared at him. "Not again! How many times do I have to tie your cravat?" He laughed. "Thirty years and three continents, and you still haven't got the hang of it." He seized Pettigrew's tie. "Hold still."

He stood back. "Now you look like the great detective that Gertrude so obviously admires." He chuckled. "Maybe she could learn to tie a cravat." He opened the room door and looked across the hall. Music floated up from below. "Let us go down to the ladies."

❧

Flinders waited at the foot of the grand staircase. He looked up and saw her, and his eyes widened.

Who is this? The apparition has become a vision.

She came down the stairs; a slender hand caressed the banister. The other held up her skirt to avoid the stair treads. A bracelet flashed. She wore a black empire gown and her rambunctious curls were smoothed into the style of Empress Eugenie. She smiled; her blue eyes opened wide.

"Ah, there you are." Flinders nodded. "Your gown is magnificent." *And so are you. What happened to the wild-looking woman with the over-sized glasses? But now that I think of it, she wasn't so wild looking after all. I have become accustomed to her.*

"I borrowed it from Gertrude."

"I see."

"From the look on your face, I take it that you approve." The blue eyes twinkled with mischief.

Am I so transparent? Pettigrew always said that my personality was exceptionally easy to read. Perhaps I should frown more and be stern like some character out of a Victorian novel.

"Where are your glasses? I thought you couldn't see without them."

"Sometimes I can, and sometimes I can't."

Flinders grinned. "Very logical. Allow me." He extended his elbow. She placed her hand on it, and they walked to the supper club. Flinders read the sign emblazoned over its door. "The Scheherazade Club. How appropriate. Perhaps Shahryar himself will show us to a table."

The glass door opened, and he entered the world of the Abbasids. Bright sound swept over him. The throb of a tawla and the clash of finger cymbals quickened his pulse. The belly dancer whirled in front of him, a cyclone of red and scarves in endless motion. The silken melody of an oud shimmered in his ears. *I am in Cairo. The dancer put her scarf around my neck and pulled me onto the floor. Her eyes never left me. We whirled and time stood still.*

And then something terrible happened.

"Somewhere discreet, I think." Flinders palmed a five-pound note.

"Of course, sir," the manager, a man in a fez, said as he bowed. "Over here. You can see, but not be seen. Please, follow me." He pulled out the chairs and they sat down.

"You stared at the belly dancer as though you were remembering something," Gazelda said, her blue eyes questioning.

"It was nothing. Something that I remembered in Cairo, many years ago."

"You were in Cairo?"

"Yes."

"I've always wanted to go." She sighed. "Did you see the Mad Caliph?"

"The Mad Caliph?"

"Yes, his name was al-Hakim. He proclaimed himself a god and turned night into day." She grinned. "They would ring bells and blow horns all night so that no one could sleep."

"Sounds unpleasant."

"Then he forbade shoemakers from making women's shoes, so women could not leave their homes."

Flinders grinned. "Possibly an excellent idea."

"You are a nineteenth-century chauvinist." Her blue eyes sparkled. "I should leave at once."

"Please do not."

"Then I will go on." Her smile hung over the table. "He would disguise himself and prowl Cairo looking for merchants who cheated their customers. His vengeance was swift."

"Swift?"

"I could describe it," she said, her blue eyes demure, "but that would be too inappropriate for a gentleman such as yourself."

"You are a font of information."

"One day he rode into the desert and disappeared."

"And so?"

"Nobody looked for him."

"How do you know all this?"

Her eyes twinkled. "I read a book while I was in the orphanage."

"A book about the Fatimids?"

"Yes. I am not pretty—boys never liked me—so I read a lot."

You are clearly mistaken about that. If I am not careful, I will become lost in those blue eyes. I will become like the Mad Caliph and disappear forever.

He turned away and examined his surroundings. The Scheherazade Club was indeed something out of *The Arabian Nights*. Moorish arches lined the walls; waiters in black and red kaftans carried trays through the room. Tapestries with Arabic script covered the walls. Men in suits and fezzes and ladies in long gowns talked and smiled.

I have seen this before.

A few turbans and kufiyahs dotted the tables. A haze of stale cigarette smoke swirled to the rhythm of the belly dancers. Silver scratched on plates, glasses clinked, and the orchestra moaned.

Yes, this could be Cairo.

Then he saw something else: unmoving tables of men in gray uniforms. They looked German. "I forgot—Gertrude told us that the new rulers were importing German military advisers." Officers' caps and an occasional spiked helmet littered their tables.

The waiter followed his eyes and whispered, "They've come down from Berlin. I think they inspected the camps."

"Camps?"

"The Armenians, you know," the waiter said as if they *should* know. Then he vanished.

Gazelda eyed the Germans. "They don't look friendly."

Flinders peered at them. "They are preparing for a war. Everybody here is preparing for a war." *Lawrence and Gertrude were also preparing at Carchemish.* A sea of monocles glinted at him. Men with close-cropped haircuts, sitting at tables, chatted and laughed. "They all look like shaving brushes standing on end," Flinders mused. "Someone should really find them a more imaginative barber. They must all smell of strong cologne and gunpowder." He shook his head. "Death wears perfume."

"Why do they prepare for war?" Gazelda asked.

"I do not know. But I have felt it coming for a long time now,"

Flinders said. He saw Gertrude and Pettigrew crossing the dining room. "Ah, here they come." He waved and beckoned. "Do sit down."

Pettigrew pulled out a chair and Gertrude sat down. They did not look at each other. Pettigrew signaled to a waiter. "A large whiskey, please."

"Make that two," Gertrude added.

Pettigrew and Gertrude studied the menu. "You never wrote," Gertrude muttered. "You do not care."

"I did not know where you were. Of course, I care."

"I remember hearing this before," Flinders whispered behind his menu. "Perhaps there is trouble in paradise."

Gazelda smiled. "I suppose the two of us bicker as much as we do get along."

"Ah, Jane Austen, is it?" Flinders chuckled.

"It appears so." Gazelda smiled. "I am quite fond of Jane Austen."

"We might as well be here alone," Flinders said. "They don't even know that we're here."

Pettigrew said, "I gave you the firman. Did you look at it?"

"I sent it to our translation department," Gertrude snapped. "They'll be quick about it."

"Another whiskey, please."

"And for me as well," Gertrude rasped.

Flinders leaned on his elbows. Clearly there was a great deal of trouble in paradise.

An orderly appeared and handed Gertrude a note. She read it and frowned. "They've found something—I have to go."

"I will go with you," Pettigrew said and pushed back in his seat.

"Are you so sure about that?" Gertrude put her napkin down. She sighed. "Well, come along, if you must."

Pettigrew gulped his whiskey.

Gazelda asked, "Where are they going?"

"That's their business." Flinders chuckled. "Ask Ms. Austen." He watched them thread their way through the tables. The belly dancer momentarily blocked Pettigrew's way. He shook his head and pushed past her.

So now we are alone.

A waiter in a red kaftan appeared at Flinders's elbow.

"Some champagne, I think." Flinders looked at Gazelda. "Is that all right?"

"Yes."

"I suppose you want to discuss the vintage?"

"No, I am sure your selection will be impeccable."

Flinders smiled. *Well, that is a small concession.* "The menu is in French," he said. "Do you want me to translate it for you?"

"I can read French, thank you."

"Really?"

"When I was in the orphanage, there was an old custodian. He had emigrated from France. He once worked at Malmaison. He taught me to speak and read French. Every morning, I would go to his small room over the school stable."

"Malmaison? The Empress's estate?"

"Yes, he tended the rose garden."

"The rose garden."

"I love roses."

"Oh." Flinders smiled. "And where did you find these roses?"

"When I was at the orphanage, I had to walk to school. It was a few blocks away. The streets were dark. Everything was black and gray. The smell of dirt and rotten food was everywhere." She sighed. "Men leered at me, and I was afraid. But at a corner, there was a flower stand." She smiled. "The color of the roses was bright pink and red against the darkness. The smell was honey in my nose."

Honey in your nose. Yes, the roses in the garden were honey in my nose as well.

Next, she will be telling me about baby finches.

Flinders hid a smile behind his menu. "The champagne is here at last."

The waiter poured two glasses. Bubbles frothed.

She turned the glass in her hand, examining it. "This is called a 'coupe,'" she said. "It has a wide rim. Do you know why?" She slid a slender finger round the rim.

"Please tell me."

She leaned forward, her eyes filled with innocence. "Louis the Fifteenth and his mistress, Madame de Pompadour, invented this shape." Her voice dropped to a whisper. "It is said to resemble her breasts."

"To resemble her breasts?"

She looked into his eyes, holding his gaze. "Yes."

"How do you know this?"

"I read it in a French history book. I read everything—I love to read."

"Indeed."

A veritable bookworm. But so was I. I sat in my room and read about the world. My father would look in at the door and say, "Flinders, ye cannae be always readin' there and daydreamin'; ye must arise and act."

"French books are difficult to read."

"But about the breasts," Flinders said and grinned.

"There is another version of the story."

"No doubt. There always is."

She arched an eyebrow. "There are those who say that it was modeled after the left breast of Marie Antoinette."

"Her left breast?" Flinders grinned behind his napkin. "This is getting out of hand. I shall never be able to look at a champagne glass again." He swirled the champagne, looked thoughtfully at the glass, and then laughed. "My world is never going to be the same."

"To Marie Antoinette."

"To Marie Antoinette."

Their glasses clinked.

The waiter brought their plates.

"This is magnificent," Flinders said, looking up at him.

"Thank you, sir. Our chef is a graduate of Le Cordon Bleu."

Flinders looked at his plate. *So now I eat food prepared by a chef trained at Le Cordon Bleu. But I am not hungry; I pick at my food. When you are with a charming woman, food is not a concern.*

The dinner was long, but neither of them ate very much. Waiters scurried about. The murmur of conversation filled the air. The belly dancers left, the orchestra played Strauss waltzes, and then the clink of glasses and chime of silver resumed.

The waiter brought a dessert menu.

"Ah-ha, they have Peach Melba." Flinders sighed. "It's my favorite dessert. Nellie Melba has a wonderful voice. I go to Covent Garden to hear her every time she comes to town. I once heard her sing as Mimi in *La Boheme*. Magnificent."

"You mean like this?" Gazelda softly hummed a melody.

"Yes, that's it." Flinders leaned forward to listen better. "Mi chiamano Mimi—they call me Mimi . . . The aria soars beyond belief."

"Beyond belief," Gazelda said and continued humming.

"More champagne?"

"Yes, please."

He filled her glass. "Hold it steady, please." Their hands touched and Flinders pretended to flinch. "Che gelida manina."

"My hands are always cold." She laughed. "The orphanage had no heat, so I wore woolen mittens."

You always wore mittens—I can see them now. The girl with the long braids put the book down and rubbed her face with a mittened hand. The mitten was too long and made her blink. She sneezed.

"I am not a tenor," Flinders said.

"And I am not a soprano."

Flinders felt his senses heighten. Snatches of conversation and laughter at far away tables suddenly roared in his ears. Silver chimed on plates like a thousand striking clocks.

He took her hand, and her fingers nestled into his palm. He pulled her to him and leaned forward.

She closed her eyes.

The sights and sounds of the cabaret faded to nothingness . . .

"Trink, trink, trink!"

Raucous laughter exploded in his ears.

His head snapped back, and her fingers disappeared.

The moment was lost. The cabaret burst into noise.

The Germans erupted into a raucous drinking song; they waved steins and swayed, singing, "Drink, drink, drink," *I know the words from my days at Oxford. Strange to hear them again in this place.* Beer splashed the floor; a spiked helmet rolled between the tables. Then the song trailed off, and the laughter faded. A solo tenor voice started singing a haunting melody. Beer steins clunked on the tables. The men in gray looked at each other and, one by one, they joined in to sing another, much softer song. They rocked back and forth, and some cried.

Flinders asked the waiter, "What are they singing?"

"They say it's a love song. It's just come out this year."

"What is it called?"

"They call it 'Lili Marleen,' and they say that it's from a German poem."

"Do you know what it's about?" Flinders asked.

"They said it was about a sentry yearning for his lost love."

A soldier, lonely on sentry duty, haunted by the vision of a woman he once loved. Are we not all haunted by such visions?

"Lili Marleen." Flinders stared. "Even these hard men have hearts." *Does their bravado hide a sense that some terrible calamity is about to befall them? I think that 'Lili' has a long way to go and will be sung by many men on their way to battle.*

I can feel the cold in my bones.

"You brood," she said. Her blue eyes were intent.

"Sometimes. I apologize—it is the Irish in me."

"The Irish in you?" Gazelda's eyes were worried. "I think that there is something more."

"I dream of visions."

"But I am flesh and blood," Gazelda said.

"Indeed you are; indeed you are."

They finished dessert.

"It is getting late and tomorrow will come all too early."

The singing trailed into silence. The clink of glasses resumed, and the orchestra played a last Strauss waltz and then began to leave.

Flinders took a last look around. The club was quiet. Empty chairs surrounded white tables littered with plates and napkins. The orchestra stand was deserted. A few couples sat with their heads close together and half-empty champagne glasses in their hands. A man in a turban with a ferocious mustache smoked a large pipe in a corner. Most of the German officers had left. The few that remained were sprawled in stupor across their tables. One leaned back in his chair. His head lolled and his tunic was unbuttoned. Officers' hats littered the floor.

Another officer caught Flinders's eye. A young lieutenant, no more than thirty, was sitting alone. His eyes were dark. A camera swung from his shoulder strap. *The lieutenant has been taking pictures.* He stared at a half-empty wine glass in front of him. *What has he seen, that he needs to blot it out with drink? He should be home eating strudel with his mother. This is no place for youthful innocence.*

Flinders carefully folded his napkin and then looked at its neat corners. *An oasis of order in a desert of disorder.*

A silent flash crossed one of the dining room's high windows.

"Is that fireworks?"

"No," the waiter said. "It is gunfire. A cognac, sir?"

"No, thank you." Flinders looked up. "Why is there gunfire in the middle of Baghdad?"

"It's the Armenians, sir." The waiter brushed some crumbs from the table. "The Special Operations are rounding them up." He handed Flinders the bill.

"Special Operations? What have they done?"

"Resisting, sir." The waiter pocketed Flinders's tip. "Armenians and other Christians have been aiding the Russians, sir."

"Other Christians?"

"Assyrians, sir." The waiter picked up the plates. "Do not worry, sir—most of the fighting is much farther north." He smiled. "You are safe here. Anything else that I can do for you?"

"Nothing. Thank you."

The waiter bowed. "Have a good night, sir."

"Yes, good night."

Flinders saw another soundless light, and then the windows went dark.

The legions stopped with a clump. Bronze-helmeted officers shouted orders. Soldiers kicked down doors and dragged women and children out of their houses. They screamed as they were pushed into carts. "They go to their deaths. What will you do about it?" Flinders shook his head and put it in his hands. *"You can do nothing but watch?" The vision faded. The voices drifted into nothingness.*

This is the world of the sword, and I must navigate it.

"Are you all right?"

He stood up. "Yes, quite all right. Come, Miss Jones, we need an early start."

She nodded, glanced briefly at the window, and then looked at Flinders. Her eyes were like question marks.

They pushed past the now empty tables. Flinders turned for a last look. The young lieutenant had not moved. An older officer pulled his hands. "Armen, Armen." The officer lifted him out of his seat and pushed him through the door.

What has he seen?

As the glass door closed behind him, he looked up at the sign. *Scheherazade, I wonder what she would think about all this? Possibly another night's tale, longer and sadder than the others?*

Another bright flash glowed briefly through the windows and faded. Flinders watched the brief glow. Then he stood up and offered Gazelda his hand.

They walked out of the dining room and into the lobby. He could feel her hips moving next to his. Chandeliers glittered; music floated in the air. Ghostlike bursts lit the lobby windows and illuminated their path. The brocade chairs were empty except for an old man with a short, white beard and dark eyes.

As Flinders and Gazelda passed, the old man winked. "Have a nice night, sir."

In the lobby, a drowsy desk clerk slumped in his chair. The statue of Isis followed them with her eyes as they climbed the broad staircase. A red carpeted hallway opened before them; the carpet was thick under their feet. Room doors floated past; their knobs glittered in the crystal light. Busts of famous men lowered their eyes and smiled. They stopped in front of the door to her room. Their eyes met, and they stood close for a shivery moment. Flinders felt the hallway around him grow breathless with anticipation. Faint music echoed from below.

He leaned forward. She stretched up. He could see only her face before him. Then he stiffened and drew back. *I cannot kiss her. I am the flying Dutchman himself, condemned to sail the world without human contact. I cannot drag her into this world.* Flinders hesitated and then extended his hand.

"Good night, Miss Jones."

She sighed.

"Good night, Mr. Petrie."

The door closed, and Flinders walked back along the hallway. It was empty; the carpet was thin under his boots. Room doors were shut in silent rebuke. Statues flowed past, solemn and unsmiling on their pedestals. He thought he heard a door open for a moment and then softly close. He whistled a melody, "'*Oh soave fanciulla*,' oh gentle maiden."

Oh gentle maiden.

I wonder.

The music soared in his mind.

Maybe there is still hope for the Dutchman. But not now, and not here in the world of the sword.

The hallway closed behind him, and the melody faded into the carpeted silence.

FIVE

The Dragoman's Revenge

"You stare at my hand, effendi."

The voice was guttural, and Flinders found the words difficult to follow.

Gertrude's office was warm in the morning. She had waved them into chairs and smiled at Pettigrew. "I want to introduce our head dragoman," Gertrude had said. "Dragomen are the eyes and ears of the British Empire. It is well known that they are 'the tongue that speaks and the ears that hear.' His name is Theopolis, but his code name is Doctor Faustus. He speaks ten languages and knows everything." She extended her hand. "Doctor."

A man stooped and wrinkled with age stood up. Flinders watched him move slowly across the room, his heavy robe trailing the floor and a long-speckled beard reaching to his waist. The robe had a fur collar, and straggles of gray hair escaped from under a large unkept turban;

chains and earrings jingled. His right hand was made of wood. The
dragoman returned Flinders's stare. He turned his bulk and looked at
Flinders through watery eyes.

"You stare at my hand, effendi," he said. "Have you never seen a
wooden hand before?"

"I'm sorry—I did not mean to stare," Flinders apologized.

"Many people stare, effendi." The dragoman knocked on the table.
"It is made of cedar, from the cedars of Lebanon. It is very hard; I
sometimes use it to crack nuts." He laughed tightly. "And it keeps
moths away."

"If I may ask, what happened to it?"

The dragoman looked surprised. "An Englishman wants to know
what happened to an old Greek?"

"I do."

"A long time ago, I was in the service of the Veiled One's family. I
served them well for many, many years. I translated for the old general.
When his father and mother were killed, the Veiled One blamed me.
He said that I had secretly contacted the sultan and betrayed them."

"And did you?"

"Of course not. The old general and I had worked together for
many years." He sighed. "I would never betray him. Someone in his
household told the sultan's men that the general was planning a coup.
The sultan struck at once."

"And was he?"

"No, it was a lie." The wooden hand rapped on the table. "The rest
you know."

"We have read the reports," Pettigrew broke in.

The dragoman rubbed the polished wood. "Several months after
the Veiled One's escape, the Bulbul captured me. He seized me around
the neck and plunged my hand into boiling oil. He hummed while
I screamed. Then he let me go and said, 'My master is merciful. He
could have had me kill you, but he told me to take only your right

hand and leave the other so that you may clean yourself.' My hand turned black and shriveled. I tried rubbing it with healing balms and soothing oils, but nothing worked." He sighed and shook his head. "One day it just fell on the floor." The watery eyes opened wide. "It lay there unmoving." He closed his eyes and bent his head. "I buried it and got this wooden hand. A wooden carving to replace flesh and blood. Look at it. Look at it!" His eyes became like hot coals. "But I have sworn revenge."

"Theopolis knows everything about the Veiled One." Gertrude's voice was a purr.

"Yes, I have watched his every move," the dragoman said. His speckled beard quivered. "I wait for the day of vengeance."

Pettigrew leaned forward in his chair. "Do you know where he is now?"

The dragoman slowly turned; his robe scratched across the floor. "He hides in an abandoned Abbasid palace on the bank of the Tigris."

"Why an abandoned palace?" Flinders asked.

"The palace complex is vast—it covers many measures of land. There are hidden places that no one has ever seen." The dragoman frowned. "You do not understand your adversary, effendis. You live in a word of reason and logic. The Veiled One lives in the tenth century of Islam. He does not see the world the way you do." He paused. "Can you understand that?"

"Yes," Flinders replied. "We once marched on Jerusalem to restore an ancient belief."

The dragoman scrutinized Flinders. "Your reputation precedes you."
"How so?"

"You are a strange man, Mr. Petrie." He shook his head. "I am told that you are an Irishman." He laughed. "Traders from the time of the Queen of Sheba have visited your island. Your heritage may be different than you think."

"I am an ordinary detective."

"I think not," he said, and the speckled beard nodded. "You search for what cannot be found. But I will help you. My right hand whispers from its grave and demands that I do."

"Please, go on."

"The Veiled One sees himself as the savior of Abbasid glory. He uses the techniques and tactics of six hundred years ago." The dragoman's eyes widened. "His assassins are from Alamut, his men are organized in brotherhoods, and his propagandists use the ancient call to revolt, the dawah itself."

"I have read about the Abbasid revolution," Flinders said. "But I thought he was only a young Turkish officer."

"After the fire where he was burned beyond belief, his mind snapped, and he became the 'Veiled One.' The name itself harkens back to stories of mysterious beings." The dragoman wheezed. "You are dealing with a phantom out of the past."

"A jinn, you mean."

"A jinn, if you will." The dragoman shook his head. "But jinns are from ancient Arabia—this phantom is from the heart of an empire."

The dragoman shivered.

"Some call him al-Shabah, The Ghost."

"Have you ever seen his face?"

"Never." The dragoman shuddered. "To do so would mean a slow and painful death."

"Theopolis has translated the paper you found," Gertrude said. "He says that it's a delivery order. They must have woven it for the Veiled One. Here is his translation. 'Deliver the bones of the kafir to the Jar of the Caliph. Knock three times and all will be revealed. Run along the balcony of bliss and place it on the throne of the golden herons. Your reward will be beyond the stars in the heavens.'"

"That is all well and good," Pettigrew said, frowning. "But how are we to find the 'Jar of the Caliph' in acres of palaces?"

"Do you know where it is?" Flinders asked the dragoman.

"I do not."

"Well, then let us adduce." Flinders steepled his hands. "Thomas, do you remember your Auguste Dupin?"

"I do. But we were very young then."

"Age does not matter—it is the analysis that counts. Thomas, we must work backward from what we know."

"And what do we know?"

"The Veiled One dreams of reviving past glory. Hence, in his madness, he would gravitate to an abandoned Abbasid palace." Flinders looked at the dragoman. "Do you agree?" "Yes, he would hide in a palace." The dragoman's eyes lit up. "The palace of Caliph al-Nasir is still intact. We call it the Qasr al-Abbasi—the Palace of the Abbasids."

"But where in the palace?" Flinders rubbed his nose. "Thomas, think back to Istanbul."

"He was hiding in a harem," Pettigrew replied.

"A harem . . . where he could imagine himself as a sultan."

"But there are no harems left in this palace."

"Are we so sure?" Flinders turned to the dragoman. "Are there empty harem quarters?"

"Yes." The dragoman nodded.

"Are any of them preserved?"

"Yes, there are still many rooms." The dragoman wheezed and then sat silent. "Many rooms, indeed."

A Marconi clacked in the distance. Somewhere, a cat meowed.

These ordinary sounds reached Flinders's ears, but his mind was somewhere else, somewhere in the distant past.

"Aha!" Flinders leaned forward and exclaimed. "We have found the answer."

"Flinders, it is still a wild goose chase." Pettigrew shook his head. "And stop saying 'aha.' You sound like Holmes."

"Not quite." Flinders waved the paper. "'Run along the Corridor of Bliss'—those are the words."

"What is the Corridor of Bliss?"

The dragoman answered. "It is a gallery where the Caliph could watch dancing girls below and choose a partner for the night. All Abbasid palaces have such a corridor."

"So the Veiled One sits in an empty palace, in an empty gallery, and watches imaginary dancers on the floor below," Flinders persisted. "We are finally getting somewhere."

"Yes."

The dragoman scratched his beard. "But the gallery and the dancers may not be imaginary."

"Perhaps Scheherazade whispers in his ear."

"Yes."

How am I so different? I sit in an empty sitting room and dream of imaginary tigers.

Pettigrew frowned. "But then he leaves the gallery and destroys people."

"Yes." The dragoman fondled his wooden hand. "He has many adherents."

"And he has the relic," Pettigrew added. He looked thoughtful.

"Yes."

"All we have to do is find the gallery," said Flinders.

"A gallery hidden behind a vanished jar?" Pettigrew shook his head.

"Thomas, we must find the Caliph's jar."

"How are you going to find a single jar in a labyrinthian palace?" Pettigrew scratched an ear. "This is not just an impossible dream—this is simply impossible."

"Nonsense." Flinders grinned. "Thomas, do you remember Bell's lectures on hidden indicators?"

"But of course."

"All we need to find are traces of recent human activity, and then follow them."

"He is right," Gazelda interjected. She had sat silently all this time. "Bell was quite emphatic about hidden indicators."

"And so was Holmes," Flinders said. "And Thomas, as I remember, you were quite good at finding subtle signs of wear at Kom al-Shoqafa."

"The Mound of Shards." Pettigrew laughed. "Yes, I made out the worn footsteps leading to Cleopatra's tomb. It comes back to me now. . . . You were about to become 'magical' and convert yourself into a magician."

"I did no such thing."

"The great Mesmer, I think," Pettigrew said. "Unfortunately, the great Mesmer was long dead."

"Did you find the tomb?" Gazelda leaned forward.

Flinders peered at her. "You ask too many questions."

Gertrude stood up. "We have a car waiting. The dragoman will go with you."

"Thank you." Flinders pushed his chair back.

"This is the second time I've been deprived of an adventure with such a stylish colleague." Gertrude fluttered her eyes at Flinders.

"Wait a minute," Flinders hesitated. "I think it would be better if Miss Jones remained here. *This is not the search of an empty shop—it is too dangerous.*

"What do you think, Thom—"

His words were abruptly cut off. Gazelda bounced in front of him. "That is absolute nonsense." Her eyes glinted and her small jaw jutted. "I'm going with you, and that's all there is to it."

Flinders folded his arms and stuck out his own chin.

I think the Americans would call this a "rhubarb." He shook his head. *Jane Eyre confronts Rochester. . . . What am I to do with this woman?* "You're not going," he said, trying out a little more firmness.

What am I supposed to do with this woman?

Flinders looked around, hoping for some support. Pettigrew

intently followed a fly as it crawled across one of the tulips in the vase behind Gertrude. Gertrude blew a smoke ring and watched it drift away. The dragoman ruffled his fur collar and blew his nose. The overhead fan hummed quietly; a typewriter bell chimed behind the office's door.

"I think I am going."

"I think not."

Gazelda shook her fist. "And I have had enough of your 'Miss Jones' nonsense. Call me by my name, or don't talk to me."

"Don't talk to you?"

"You heard me."

There was a small woman, once. She wore white and said, "I am pharaoh of Egypt, and I do not bend to the might of Rome."

And now, I confront another.

Pettigrew rubbed his own jaw to hide a smile and then drawled, "It does seem as though the matter is settled, Flinders."

Gertrude stifled a grin. The dragoman sneezed. Footsteps passed in the hall outside; the steps drummed on the bare floor. The fly circled the tulips.

"Give up, Flinders," Pettigrew said and chuckled.

It seems so. But I will worry about her. "All right, I surrender. The matter is settled; she will go."

Wellington once said, "It is a wise general who knows when to retreat." But Wellington did not have to deal with such a stubborn woman.

A Marconi clicked and thumped to a stop. Somewhere, typewriters chattered to each other. The fly buzzed and flew through a window.

Gertrude opened another file and read. "Leave now, but hurry back. Young Toynbee says that there are reports of mobs. They are burning and looting parts of the city." She looked at them. "Young Toynbee says that they are headed this way. The old Ottoman order is breaking down here in Baghdad." She pursed her lips. "We really can't defend this installation."

"Who is young Toynbee?" Flinders asked.

"A bright young man on loan from the Foreign Office. He is studying the history of the region. He is most concerned about violence against the Armenians." She laughed. "You would like him, Mr. Petrie—he is a lot like you." She arched an eyebrow. "But not as elegant, of course."

"I thought Father Christmas was in charge of field reports," said Flinders.

"He is, but he is on holiday in the Seychelles."

"On holiday in the middle of a crisis?"

"Yes, Father Christmas is a bird fancier, and the Seychelles are home to many rare species."

"A bird fancier." Flinders shook his head. "How foolish of me. I should have known."

"You do not understand." Gertrude sighed. "We are governed by strict Civil Service rules. Tea must be served promptly at four, we dress formally for dinner, and personal holidays are scrupulously honored."

"I've had the tea. It was in the morning." He smiled. "Beautifully done. But dressing formally for dinner?"

"That is really our local custom," Gertrude explained. "The previous ambassador was a stickler for formality. He always dressed for dinner."

"Please do go on; this is becoming fascinating."

"One evening, a riot broke out and a mob stormed the embassy. Father Christmas was putting on his studs and cuff links when the mob smashed through the gates and charged the compound. The melee was terrible. People were getting hit over their heads, and bullets flew everywhere. He straightened his cuffs, picked up his pistol, went downstairs, and started shooting at the rioters." Gertrude chuckled. "They were eventually driven off. Then he said, 'Dammy, I think I've lost a cuff link. I will have to find another set. And I suppose my dinner is now cold, as well.'"

Flinders laughed. "A man after my own heart. You must dress the part so your adversaries know who you are and your friends respect your resolve."

"Yes. So we honor his memory by dressing for dinner."

But will the Veiled One respect my resolve?

Pettigrew grinned.

Gazelda shook her head. "First children's books, now dressing for dinner."

"Now off you go, and don't dawdle. I must prepare to evacuate. We will move to the embassy. It's fortified and has a detachment of Royal Marines." Gertrude smiled. "And the new government well knows how His Majesty feels about people who attack his embassies."

They stood up to go.

"Wait." Gertrude reached into a cabinet and pulled out a pistol. "This is a machine pistol. It is small in caliber but extremely deadly. We use it at close range—for special occasions." She handed the pistol to Gazelda. "Use it well."

The car with the blue headlights ground to a stop. Noonday sun blazed off its hood. A cat stared at its occupants from behind a stone fountain. Flinders looked up at the gray walls. Pigeons sat listlessly on the parapets. "Are these all that's left of the Abbasids?"

"I do not think so, effendi." The dragoman smiled. "The Abbasids are already in your mind. Scheherazade leans close and speaks softly to you. You hear and you dream about princes and princesses and a world of adventure and magic." He looked at Flinders. "Is that not what brings you here, effendi?"

"You speak of a golden age."

"Yes, a golden age that haunts us forever."

A golden age. Kudret said that the golden age of the Ottomans was the Tulip era. The dragoman says that the golden age of the Arabs was the Abbasid Caliphate. What is my golden age? Is it the land of the far pavilions that gleam gold and silver in the setting sun? Or is it this dusty street where I and my friends prepare to enter an Abbasid palace and confront a monster?

"Well, golden age or not, we still have to get inside."

"The Mongols destroyed most of this palace, but they could not breach these walls. No one knows what they hide."

"Is there an entrance?"

"Yes." The dragoman drew a sleeve across his nose.

"The dust, you know; it makes me sneeze." Then he pointed. "Over there is a fissure in the walls. It is wide enough to slip through. When I was a boy, I would crawl through it and climb the stairs to the Corridor of the Caliphs." He laughed. "They say the palace is haunted. Everyone is afraid to enter."

"Corridor of the Caliphs?" Flinders said, getting out of the car.

"All Abbasid palaces have them. They have hidden doors and peepholes, so the Caliphs could watch in secret." The dragoman smiled. "You may walk in the footsteps of Harun al-Rashid himself." He chuckled. "Beware if you hear the rustle of silk, effendis."

They crossed the street. Donkey carts rattled past them. A pigeon swooped in front of them. The dragoman called out, "I will sit in the shade, eat my shawarma, and doze until you come back." He unwrapped a large sandwich. "Have you ever eaten shawarma, effendi?"

Flinders nodded. "Yes, I have."

"I would have thought it too spicy for your European taste."

"No, effendi," Flinders said. *I ate shawarma before going into the baths of Cleopatra. Now he speaks of shawarma again before I enter the palace of Scheherazade.*

The dragoman chuckled. "You learn swiftly, my friend."

They squeezed through the jagged opening. Pale light and cool air greeted them after the blare and heat of the street. The silence was oppressive. Rough stone stairs circled a stone pillar and disappeared into darkness above. "This appears to be an old cistern," Flinders said, looking up and down. "Yes, I think I can catch the glint of waves below. That is the Tigris."

"It's as though we are in another world," Gazelda said. It was so still that Flinders thought that he could sense her shivering.

"We have stepped into the past," Flinders whispered.

"There are stairs," Pettigrew said. "We must climb them."

"Stay close to the walls," Flinders said. "It's a long way down."

"I think I'm going to be dizzy."

"Do not be dizzy. Dizziness is unhelpful." Flinders handed her a flashlight. "Use this to see."

The three climbed upward; when Flinders peered over his shoulder, he could see their shadows moving uneasily behind them. They reached the top and stood on a narrow landing.

"Stairs cannot end at a blank wall," Pettigrew said. "Flinders, see if you can find some sort of spring."

Flinders ran his light along the uneven stones. "There is a small indentation here. I can see its edges in the light." He pushed the stone. "It gives way."

The wall ground open to reveal a narrow corridor. Flecks of plaster fell on its floor. Flashlight beams penciled across its gray walls. Flinders stepped through the opening and into the corridor. "It's narrow and high. I can see an arched roof. There's a cold draft."

"Of course." Gazelda nodded. "The Abbasids engineered their palaces to produce cooling airways."

"Another book?" Flinders said.

"Indeed so."

Pettigrew ran his light along the walls. "There are alcoves bounded by pillars leading to side passages. I cannot see the end of the corridor." He looked down. "The tiles are dusty. This place has been undisturbed for centuries."

"Are you so sure?" Gazelda sniffed. "I smell something that is not dust. But I can't make it out."

"Are you sure it is not the smell of centuries-old silk rustling behind you?" Flinders flashed his light around the walls.

"Ghosts do not smell."

"How do you know?"

"I have it on the highest authority," Gazelda replied.

"Highest authority?" Flinders arched an eyebrow.

"Henry James, of course."

"Ah, you have been reading *The Turn of the Screw*." Pettigrew shook his head. "Someone is watching us, most probably with deadly intent, and you two discuss Gothic horror stories."

"You started all this in the weaver's alley." Gazelda grinned.

"I bow my head in shame." Flinders knelt. "Anyway, you may be right. There is something—I can see faint disturbances in the dust." He sniffed. "No, I don't smell anything but dust."

"Perhaps my imagination," Gazelda said softly.

They walked cautiously down the corridor. Their flashlights danced on the walls. Hints of gold flashed in the beams. The silence weighed heavy on Flinders. "Wait!" He stopped. "I hear a bird."

Pettigrew said, "Yes, that is the same sound that was in the Krak des Chevaliers."

"Someone is watching us," said Flinders.

"Clearly."

Flinders moved closer to Gazelda and Pettigrew. Chirps followed them.

They drew their pistols.

"Should I tell a joke to break the tension?"

"A joke?" Flinders looked at Gazelda. "What*ever* are you talking about?"

"Yes, I believe you said that babbling was necessary to keep us relaxed and ready for action."

"I did say something of the sort." Pettigrew nodded.

"Don't encourage her," Flinders hissed.

"Nonsense, let's hear it," Pettigrew said.

Gazelda smiled. "Then I will proceed. One morning, Holmes came out of the flat and found Watson standing on the corner with a revolver in one hand and a knife in the other. 'Why are you standing like that?' Holmes asked. Watson replied, 'Because I don't know whether to shoot down the alley or cut across the street.'"

"You made that up," Flinders said, tapping her arm with his flashlight. "Watson would never do such a thing."

"How do you know?"

"Watson was a pillar of the community, that's how I know."

"Enough silliness," Pettigrew growled. "Speaking of pillars . . ." He pointed. "There looks to be a smudge on this one. Possibly part of a handprint. Would you take a look?"

"Indeed so." Flinders sniffed. "There is a faint smell, as well."

"Gazelda, would you lend us your educated nose?"

She sniffed. "Baghdad Gold."

"The same as in the weaver's shop."

"The hashshashin."

Pettigrew nodded.

"That reminds me." Flinders chuckled. "Did I ever tell you about the curator my uncle pawned off on Budge? 'A regular curating bloodhound,' Uncle said. He could sniff out a forgery from twenty paces away. He specialized in Vermeers—something about the oils Vermeer used. Anyway, he was a fraud, and Budge was furious."

"Furious about a nose?" Pettigrew laughed.

"Stop that, both of you," Gazelda said.

Another chirp echoed in the empty hall.

"The handprint is fresh." Flinders peered at it.

"How do you know?" Gazelda peered at the print.

"There is dust on the pillar, but none on the print." Flinders smiled. "You have much to learn."

Dust swirled as they moved. Rows of pillars shifted and wavered as they passed. Shadows dappled the walls behind them. A rat squeaked across the dust. "I think we are in luck," Pettigrew said. "If there are rats, then there is food. There would be no rats if the palace was abandoned."

Flinders nodded. "Yes, there are humans close by. The rat would not be far from its source of food."

"Besides, rats do not chirp," Gazelda offered.

"You are correct, Gazelda." Flinders ran his flashlight along the walls. "I see slots in the walls. The Caliph could see into every room." He flicked the beam. "Thomas, how terrifying to be a counsellor and know that the Caliph could watch you at any time."

Pettigrew nodded. "Yes, and execute you at any time."

"Scheherazade does not say anything about this," Gazelda said, frowning.

"Of course not. She was Shahryar's wife." Flinders paused. *Mariam said that Scheherazade was a myth, and that* The Arabian Nights *were Abbasid propaganda tales designed to create the image of a golden age. Maybe so, but these tales have moved imaginations for centuries.* He shook his head. *But these walls are real. This palace is real. This danger is real.* "Keep moving—and be alert," he told them.

A faint draft of cold air struck Flinders's cheek as he passed one of the arches. He stopped and looked down at the short passage. It ended in a blank wall. He sniffed. "Jasmine, I wonder." He sniffed again. "You two go on; I want to look at something. I'll catch you up in a minute."

He walked down the passage. "Aha, there is an enclave that you cannot see from the corridor, and there is a tall jar." He examined the wall. "But there are no cracks that I can see or feel." He knelt. "Nothing down here either, but I can feel a draft and the jasmine smell is stronger."

A draft and no visible cracks—it is not possible. Holmes once said, "When you eliminate the impossible, whatever remains must be the truth." There must be an entrance.

He stood up. "The order said to knock three times." He knocked on the wall. "Nothing." He knocked in a different place. "Again, nothing." He thought for a long moment. "For Holmes, this would not even be a one-pipe problem." He scratched his head. "I am overlooking something obvious." He pulled an ear and then smiled. "How stupid to miss that! The order said to deliver the relic to the Jar of the Caliph. The knock was supposed to be on the jar."

He rapped on the jar. A hollow rumble vibrated in its depths and the entire wall slowly revolved to reveal a narrow gallery.

Jasmine overpowered him.

"The Balcony of Bliss!"

Flinders beamed his light into the opening. The gallery was dark and cramped. Rotten benches lined one side; a mashrabiyah screen ran along the other. Flinders looked through the latticework. Below him, a tiled courtyard spread out. Small fountains, now dry, lined the floor. Soft light from some opening high above played over the tiles. Jasmine filled the air; streams of rose petals covered the floor.

Here is where the Caliph sat and picked out a woman for the night. Flinders studied the floor. "The rose petals are traced in regular patterns. Someone has been dancing on this floor." *I read an old tale out of* The Arabian Nights. *Two women were picked out for the Caliph's pleasure. They were made to sit over slow fires burning rose petals until they were sufficiently scented. Then they were taken to the Caliph.*

What kind of men would treat women only as objects of desire?

Flinders ran his flashlight along the pitted floor. There were footprints in the dust. *And here is a cushion—quite new, I think. The Veiled One is not far.* The balcony ended with a curtained doorway.

Flinders followed the footprints and stepped through the curtain into bright light.

"May I help you, effendi?" The voice was cold with menace.

Flinders looked up. The Veiled One stood in front of him. A smaller shadow stood behind. A silver veil covered the cold face. Flinders could see only two yellow eyes that blazed with hate. He wore a black robe and held a saber. "I have been expecting you for some time, now." The eyes stared over the silver links. "I have watched you and your friends follow my steps ever since that foolish priest hired you." The veil smiled and pointed.

"You want the bones, well there they are."

Flinders saw a small throne. Golden herons circled its seat, and an ivory casket sat on its gold cushion. *The casket is smaller than I imagined. How could something so small be so great?*

"Great caliphs sat on this throne a thousand years ago. Now I sit on it and seek vengeance. The world will tremble before me as it did before them. But the seat is empty; the bones rest on it. All you have to do is come and get them."

"That is all I have to do?"

"Your blonde companion killed my only friend," the veil snarled. "And you carried off my mother's memory." *I saw her picture.* "You have offended me beyond belief." The veil sparkled with anger. "I have sworn to take your head and put it in a jar of honey. Maybe I will scent it with rosewater, and have my women dance before it. And I will laugh and spit on your frightened face forever." The veil pointed. "There is a saber—pick it up and face me."

Flinders saw the blade leaning against the throne.

"Your friend was lucky when he struck down the Bulbul. Now let us find out if you can do the same to me."

"We will soon see," Flinders said. He picked up the saber and strode to attack.

The Colosseum was a blinding white. A roar shook the building as he stepped out of the latticed gate. He looked up to see tier upon tier of gleaming marble surrounding him; the blue sky was bright between the dark shapes of the awnings. The heat from the sand slapped his face. Black birds circled in the sun's blaze.

He saluted.

The audience stood and cheered, rank upon rank up to the last rows. Feet stomped. Noise from the cheering crowd deafened him; they called his name, again and again. Fierce energy swept over him; the chants were thunderclaps in his ears. The sand was pristine in front of him; the air was a bright crystal in his eyes. He was haloed in light.

He looked at the faces rising above him.

"A man might well choose to die here in glory."

The sand crunched under his feet; the sword was light in his hand. A tiger padded up an open ramp. The tiger faced him, its yellow eyes never leaving him.

His blade sparkled in the sun as he raised it.

The Veiled One slashed at him. The yellow eyes fixed on his. Flinders parried and drove home. *The crowd screamed.* Chain mail blunted his thrust. The Veiled One staggered. *The crowd cried for the finish; women leaned over the parapets, their scarves fluttering in the sun. The chant swelled and repeated. "Kill him, kill him."* Flinders blocked a counterstroke. Blades clanged; sparks flashed. Flinders beat the opposing blade and lunged. His blade bent into an arc but did not penetrate the man's mail shirt.

The Colosseum shook. Drink servers stopped moving in the aisles.

Flinders swung at the Veiled One's head. Steel grated on steel. *Women screamed in frenzy, "Kill him, kill him."*

The crowd's chant rose to fever pitch.

"Kill him! Kill him!"

The world turned red with anger. The saber became a living thing in his hand, darting this way and that, eager for the kill.

"Kill him! Kill him!"

Thousands of feet pounded on marble; thousands of hands clapped.

"Kill him! Kill him!"

Flinders flicked a couple of beats on the Veiled One's blade and then slashed at his legs. A low parry blocked the blow. They closed in, both sabers intertwined, their bodies struggling back and forth.

Voices screamed.

"Kill him! Kill him!"

Rage drifted in red clouds across his eyes.

A mailed elbow struck the side of Flinders's head. The earth turned sideways. *Frozen figures slid across his vision: their eyes wide, their mouths open. Wine cups floated in midair. Black birds hung motionless in a dwindling tunnel of light above him.* The ground rose up and hit his back. His blurry eyes saw the Veiled One towering above him; his saber was raised in both hands for the final stroke. It shimmered as it moved.

"*No!*" Gazelda's shriek pierced his ear. Machine pistols chattered. The hazy figure of the Veiled One staggered and clutched its side; then it turned and disappeared. The smaller figure ran toward him and then vanished.

"Get him!" Pettigrew's shout burbled like water.

Then came darkness. Flinders heard no more.

Two blue eyes stared into his. The eyes were upside down.

"Your head is heavy. Would you like to sit up?"

"I failed." The words came slowly from Flinders's lips.

"You did not. He wore chain mail—you hit him many times."

The world came back into focus.

"But he got away."

"His chain mail stopped my bullets, but he will be very sore."

"You may rest assured that he will be back." Pettigrew's head appeared beside the blue eyes.

"I thought there was another one, a hashshashin. What happened to him?"

"There was, but no more." Pettigrew smiled. "He took a couple of swipes at me with his knife. So I picked up a bronze vase and hit him on the arm until he dropped it. Then I hit him on the head with it and he fell into a heap." He chuckled. "After a minute or two, he wobbled to his feet, so I picked him up and threw him against the wall. There was a great thump—very satisfying. He started to get up again, so I kicked him in the face." Pettigrew examined his foot. "I think one of his teeth got stuck in my boot."

"Savate, I suppose."

"Indeed so. It pays to practice." Pettigrew grinned. "The Veiled One really should recruit larger henchmen."

"My jaw hurts," Flinders told them.

"I am not surprised," Pettigrew said.

"That reminds me of a joke," Gazelda said.

"Another joke?" Flinders groaned. "Here I am almost dead, and you want to make jokes."

"You are getting stuffy in your old age." Pettigrew felt Flinders's jaw. "And you are clearly not almost dead."

"My jaw is broken."

"For a man with a broken jaw, you manage to talk quite a bit. Now be quiet and listen. I may have found a worthy protégé."

Gazelda began. "A lorry and a car collided. The car driver jumped out, took a pose, and shouted, 'Kung Fu!' The lorry driver also jumped out, shouted, 'Spanner!' and hit him in the head with it."

Pettigrew smiled in approval. "Quite so, quite so."

Flinders shook his head. "Another Pettigrew. The world isn't ready for this."

Pettigrew and Gazelda put their arms around Flinders and dragged him back down the Balcony of Bliss. "Wait!" he protested. "Where are the bones? We have forgotten the bones."

Gazelda smiled. "You worry too much. Think of the great Thurston."

"The great Thurston—what nonsense."

"Not nonsense." Gazelda grinned. "Now you see it, now you don't."

"You have the relic."

"I do." She held it out.

"You are indeed a witch."

"Witches have their moments."

They crawled back through the opening and into the street.

The sun had slipped behind the spired skyline. Shadows crept across the street like the fingers of an unseen hand. Flinders's eyes gradually focused, and he made out the figure of the dragoman sitting in the car. The dragoman waved. The sounds of voices and animals were loud in Flinders's ears after the silence of the palace.

"I'm beginning to feel like my old self."

"Are you so sure?" Gazelda's voice was a purr. "You look a little bilious."

"Possibly a touch of the catarrh." Pettigrew winked and then helped him into the car. "Perhaps a few drops of holy water might help."

"Never mind that." Flinders slammed the car door. "We must leave at once."

"Not so fast, effendis." The dragoman leaned out of the car to look around. "Did you meet the Veiled One?"

"We did."

"And did you kill him?" The dragoman's eyes were hard as he turned to look at Flinders. "My right hand listens from its grave."

"We did not," Flinders replied, "but we severely wounded him. There were blood splashes where he fled."

"Blood splashes . . ." The dragoman frowned. "That is not enough—my hand demands more."

"That is all I can tell you."

"I will kneel at its grave and ask forgiveness for you. You tried and that is enough for now. But the vengeance is not complete." He rubbed the wooden hand. Then he opened the car door. "You are right—we must leave. Get on with it, driver." Flinders grabbed the windscreen. The car with the blue headlights screeched and jolted away.

The dragoman clutched his turban. "This is much too fast for an old man."

"Nonsense. You'll get used to it in nothing flat." Flinders stretched out in his seat. "This reminds me of the races at Le Mans. Someday, they may become famous."

"Flinders, there are no races at Le Mans," Pettigrew said. "There are just road cars. Le Mans is a sleepy village."

"Thomas, you have no imagination."

A startled donkey brayed and clopped out of the way. Clouds of pigeons circled upward. Vendors spilled their wares and yelled in anger. Tires scraped on cobblestones.

Flinders saw a dark line stretching across the narrow street. "Turn the car—the way is blocked."

A rock hit the windscreen.

The dragoman moaned.

"This way driver," Flinders said.

Awnings blurred past.

"Faster, driver."

Another rock bounced off the hood.

"No, not that way, driver!"

The brakes screeched and the car tilted.

The dragoman muttered a prayer.

"Turn around the fountain, driver. Quickly, now—this street is clear."

A line of ducks flapped out of the car's path.

"Go, go!" Flinders clutched the dashboard. "I see it now." He waved. "The straightaway toward the finish line. Driver, pour it on."

The dragoman covered his eyes.

"I should have brought my scarf and goggles," Flinders said.

"You don't have a scarf and goggles," Pettigrew snapped.

"Details."

Gazelda hung on to her seat. "Does he always act like this?"

"Flinders craves excitement."

"And you?"

"In my way."

"Is there no way to tame him?"

Pettigrew studied her. "You might as well try to tame the wind."

"Tame the wind?"

"Flinders once said that a man was nothing more than temporarily arrested energy."

"Arrested energy?"

Pettigrew added, "But you cannot arrest energy. You have to accept its flow or be destroyed by it."

"I see."

"I hope so."

The street widened and the car moved quickly. Flinders turned to look behind. "There is smoke, and I can see flames. The city is burning."

"The Mongols have returned," the dragoman moaned. "Hulagu will kill us all."

"This is not the thirteenth century—these mobs are directed by someone," Flinders growled.

The car lurched to a stop in front of the spiked gate. A guard rushed them into the compound. Orderlies wheeled barrows of paper to small fires, which dotted the courtyard. *They are burning everything.* The heavy door closed behind them.

Pandemonium greeted them. Flinders saw frantic people running back and forth. Boxes broke open, and papers littered the air. Smoking stands rolled back and forth and spread cigarette butts and ashes. His boots crunched on broken glass. Office doors yawned open; splintered furniture sprawled on floors. Framed paintings hung sadly awry, and posters drooped off walls. Smoke from courtyard fires drifted across ceilings.

"This way!" a guard yelled.

Gertrude appeared from an office. Her face was drawn, and her red hair straggled down her cheeks. "We have brought in every agent nearby. Their families are with them. The rest have gone into hiding."

Pettigrew frowned. "Are you all right?"

"Yes, Thomas."

"I worry."

"Thank you, Thomas."

She pushed them into a large office. "Wait here."

Stale sweat greeted them. The room was packed with fear. Flinders crowded in, and Pettigrew and Gazelda squeezed against him. Tension slapped him in the face. The acrid smell of fear was overwhelming. Men held their wives. Children wailed. Valises sat open on the floor; combs and bracelets lay among the clothes. A pet bird fluttered nervously from shoulder to shoulder.

A small boy whispered to his mother, "Are we going to die?"

The mother wrapped her shawl around him. "Not yet, not yet."

People crowded together as more arrivals pushed into the room.

Flinders saw a group of boys dressed in red sitting in a corner of the room. "Those are koceks. What are they doing here?"

Gertrude spoke from behind him. "Kudret is here with his remaining koceks. Most have been killed—these are still alive. Kudret, where are you?"

"I am here, Gertrude." Kudret stood up. "I am always here."

Flinders pushed through the unhappy crowd and hugged Kudret. He was older now and looked tired. The once-smooth face was wrinkled, and the black hair had gray streaks. "Tell me what happened after we left."

"When the sultan was overthrown," Kudret said, "everything changed. Koceks were no longer wanted. They were killed or tortured. They scattered to their villages and hid in fear. These boys are all that is left." Kudret's eyes were sad. "We fled for our lives."

"These are all?"

"The koceks once held an empire together—now they huddle in this room."

"Where did you go?"

"My children were taken to an Assyrian monastery outside of Mosul. The Assyrians call it 'Umm al-Ahzan'—'Mary, Mother of Sorrows'— and it became the mother of my koceks." He frowned. "A well-fitting name. It is a time of sorrows for us." Then he smiled. "Strange that such a place would welcome koceks, boys who dance for men, but it did. Priests comforted them, and nuns fed them."

"Monasteries are places of worship and contemplation," Flinders said gently.

Kudret sighed. "The old empire had many strange and wondrous things. I will miss it." His eyes were wide with pain. "What a loss. Its magnificence can never be replaced." He shook his head. "The boys danced for the nuns. They cheered and applauded—they brought out tambourines and beat the rhythm. Then they said, 'It's time you were in bed' and covered the boys with blankets."

He smiled at the thought, hard lines forming around his mouth.

"In the mornings, when the sun came up," he continued, "the bell-ringer would let the boys ring the great bells. Their peals would echo off the mountains, and the boys would laugh. Then they would play soccer with the young priests and help the nuns feed the chickens." He laughed. "The boys never could beat the priests. Finally, the priests took them aside and said, 'Let us teach you how to play soccer.' I even considered becoming a priest." His eyes widened. "Imagine, my friend, a kocek studying to become a priest."

Flinders laughed. "I have heard of such things."

"My boys grew happy, their thinness became weight, and their pinched faces became round. I became a doting father when I looked at them. I heard them laugh and play in the sun, and my heart grew warm." He looked at Flinders. "Do you know what I mean, Englishman?"

"I do, indeed."

"Think of it, my friend." Kudret's face saddened, and he wrung his wrinkled hands. "That such a man could become a doting father."

"Doting fathers smile across the centuries."

"The sun was bright; the boys were happy." Kudret sighed. "And I was happy. It was a time of peace, but it did not last."

"What happened?"

"The monastery was attacked. Now the bells and the laughter are silent." Kudret looked out into space. "We fled into the mountains and found our way here."

Flinders placed a hand on Kudret's elbow. "This is a time of sorrow for all of us," he offered.

"The empire has vanished."

"Yes." He gripped the elbow, steadying Kudret. Or at least that was how it seemed.

"Everything has been destroyed. The greatness is gone, and even the tulip sellers have disappeared." Kudret shook his head. "My tulips are gone—my life is gone."

"Where is Osman?" Flinders asked, trying to distract him. "I do not see him."

Kudret looked surprised. "After all these years, you still remember a small boy in a tavern on the Street of the Women?"

"I remember the 'night of the young camels,' and I felt his pain," Flinders said. "What man could forget?" He remembered what Osman had said: *The shears were cold.*

"No man," Kudret nodded. "Osman returned to his village. He lives there with his aging parents and tends their flocks." Kudret looked to the ground. "I saw him not long ago. He seemed happier." Kudret smiled sadly. "Remember, effendi, 'the light of the day blots out the terrors of the night.' Osman now lives in the light of day."

"But now we are here."

Gertrude entered and waved for silence. "Mobs roam the streets—they shout, 'Death to the unbelievers.'" She pointed. "There is a way out. The Mamluks built an escape tunnel centuries ago. It leads to a landing on the river. We have electrified it. Barges will carry us. A gunboat will accompany us to the embassy dock. You will all be safe, but we must hurry."

A panicked murmur arose among the crowd.

"The Dutch Consulate has been set on fire," Gertrude added over the din. "It is two midans away. There is not much time."

Orderlies pushed the crowd out of the room. Babies cried. Clothes spilled on the floor. A baby's rattle rolled aimlessly among the shirts and dresses. Men and women staggered into the hall and formed a ragged line, a line of despair that inched forward in fits and halts.

Kudret hugged one of the boys. "You must go, my son, but remember me." The boy put his arms around Kudret's shoulders.

"Father."

"Father?" the Englishman questioned.

Kudret looked up. "Perhaps you and Gertrude misunderstood." He laughed. "Every morning, I shave very closely. It is a habit from my days as a kocek."

He overheard our conversation on the embassy stairs.

Kudret pushed the boys toward the hall. The boy he had hugged waved goodbye.

Muffled pounding echoed through the hall.

"You must go," Flinders urged them. "I will follow."

The room cleared. Pettigrew and Gazelda left. Flinders could hear footsteps and crying in the hall. Sad valises crumpled on the floor. The bird twittered and flew out the door.

Flinders watched as Kudret shoved the last boy through the door. "They are too slow," Kudret said. "The boats take too long to load. They will be trapped and die."

Pounding shattered the air. Heavy thuds shook the walls.

The moment of truth is at hand.

"They are here! They have broken into the courtyard," Kudret said.

He pushed Flinders toward the great door. "I will entertain our visitors for a while. That will give them some time. Come, I need your help."

They reached the great door. It groaned under the blows. Dust spurted from cracks in the wood. Its slats quivered and its hinges creaked.

"It won't last much longer," Flinders said.

"Don't worry, we have time. The Mamluks built well. Now, I must dress the part." Kudret laughed to himself. "A kocek must always look impressive."

"And so must a knight," Flinders said. "Which you very much are."

Kudret reached into the pile of clothing and pulled out a red jacket. "A little small, but it will do." He rummaged around. "I need a cap." He found one and put it on. "Flinders, there are some bracelets over there. Please hand me them." He put them on his wrists. "I need a necklace."

"The knight arms himself."

"Ha!" Kudret released a tense laugh.

"Let me look. I think I saw some over there."

Flinders searched in the piles of clothing and then held up a necklace. "It also seems small."

"It will do."

"I broke my necklace in the harem."

"Yes, I remember." Kudret smiled. "Your sword was poetry in motion. As I watched you, I felt that I was sitting at the feet of a great diwani poet. The verses and the emotion overwhelmed me." Kudret sighed. "But those verses are no more. The diwani poets are gone. My world is gone, and I must go with it." Kudret put on the necklace. "There is no face powder, and there is no kohl for my eyes. I shall have to go as I am." He looked at his reflection in a cracked door pane.

"Do you think my eyes are too small?"

"Your eyes are like the rays of the sun on an early morning." Tears pricked at his own eyes, but he held them back.

"The rays of the sun . . . I knew you were a diwani poet, my friend."

"I think that I am ready."

"How do I look?"

"Magnificent, as always."

I cannot bear this.

"Flinders, we will drink raki together."

"We will drink raki."

"And there will be tulips."

"Always tulips."

Always tulips.

"Thank you. Now please, open the door. This old kocek has one more dance left."

"Kudret, you do not have to do this." Flinders reached out and gripped his arm.

"My friend . . ." Kudret's voice was soft. "It is well said that a man is remembered not only by how he lived but also by how he died."

It is well said.

"You do not have to die," Flinders said. "The boys are well down the tunnel."

"Not far enough, my friend. Not far enough." Kudret smiled. "I am father to them all, so I have no choice. They will kill everyone. What I do will give all of you time to escape."

"Kudret, no."

"I have destroyed too many lives. Allow me this one act of atonement." He hugged Flinders and then pushed him away. "Now please—open the door."

Flinders nodded. "Forgive me for what I do," he said.

He pulled the bolts, and the door opened. Bright fire and furious noise swept in. Kudret stepped out; his red figure etched against the light of torches.

The knight takes the field.

"Remember me."

"I will."

Flinders closed the door and bolted it.

The roar stopped. Laughter broke out. Laugh upon laugh echoed in the night. Flinders ran down the deserted hallway. Its typewriters were silent. Posters of suspected spies swayed as he passed in front of them. Smoking stands filled with cigarette butts stood like abandoned sentries. His feet slipped on crumpled folders as he passed office doors—doors that gaped like toothless mouths.

The laughs behind him became fainter as he ran.

Then he stopped and listened.

The laughs turned to screams.

The knight had fallen.

The floor rocked like the deck of a ship in a high sea as he ran. Walls opened and closed like oriental screens folding and unfolding. Overhead lights blinked white and black. Scowling faces jumped off posters and floated in the air in front of him. Yellow eyes looked out from an empty office. He imagined the swish of a tail in the gloom.

A faint cry caught his ear. He looked in an office and saw a forlorn cat sitting on crumpled folders.

"Come on!" Flinders scooped it up. "You're coming with me."

Muffled screams echoed behind him. Blows thundered on the great door. He heard a heavy crash and then shouting. Footsteps thudded. *They've broken in!* He reached the tunnel door and pulled it open; green walls opened before him. Faint torchlight streamed in from behind. He slammed the door behind him, the torchlight disappeared, and the noise became a distant murmur. Bare light bulbs streamed over his head.

The bell on the cat's collar jingled as he ran.

He reached the end of the tunnel, passed through a dripping iron grating, and climbed down slick stone steps. The last barge was waiting. Pettigrew stood on its edge. He reached out to take Flinders's hand.

"Jump in!"

Gazelda's face was pale with worry.

She took Flinders's hand and clutched it.

"Che gelida manina."

"Yes." She managed a wan smile. "Very cold tonight."

Torchlight spilled on the steps behind them as the barge moved into the river's stream. The moon scudded behind a line of clouds and the river turned from silver to lead. The barges drifted silently with the current; the outlines of their passengers were black against the water. Dark lights from the fires reflected off the river's swell. A snatch of verse from Byron bubbled in Flinders's mind. *And the sheen of their spears was like stars on the sea.* The gray ghost of the gunboat slid behind them; the throb of its engines purred softly across the chill water. Damp air smelling of fish blew across their faces.

Some passengers cried softly.

Nothing seemed to move.

Gunshots crackled; explosions swelled red and then faded into a cloudy orange haze. The echo carried across the current. "We are like a painted ship on a painted ocean," Flinders muttered. "We are sailors frozen in time."

Something soft bumped the barge, and Flinders looked over the side. Sightless eyes stared up at him from two white faces. "They've been tied together and left to drown!" Heads bobbed in the swell; fire-light etched their wet shapes. "Now they have floated to the surface."

He looked across the water. "There must be hundreds of them."

He pushed Gazelda. "Stay back!"

Pettigrew grabbed the railing and leaned out. "We are sailing on a river of corpses."

We drift down the Styx itself, and the ferryman beckons before us. Flinders stared at pale faces. *Yes, a painted ship on a painted ocean. But this ocean is an ocean of lifeless heads.* Flinders muttered, "We are sailors frozen in time."

"Not quite." Pettigrew pointed at two bright lights twinkling ahead of them. "I can see the embassy's dock."

Cones of bright light danced across the dark water. Heads bobbed white circles in the watery halos.

A gray moth crawled across the windscreen. Its motion caused Flinders to open his half-closed eyes; he had been daydreaming. He watched it flutter its wings and then become still. He felt, rather than saw, the small eyes looking at him. The car with the blue headlights crept along the desert road. Its lights were out, except for the low sidelights. Pettigrew and Gazelda dozed in the back seat. Flinders looked from side to side. The desert was dark except for the narrow tunnel of rutted road that unrolled before them. Clumps of desert sage streamed under the car and disappeared.

His mind returned to the scene at the embassy, hours before.

The barges had thumped into the dock, the passengers tumbling across the wooden ramp and onto the wet dock. Dark pools of water mirrored red from the fires on shore. Flinders imagined he was running across a sea of flames. They rushed into the embassy; the heavy door slammed, and the fire disappeared. Orderlies led them to food and rooms.

Gertrude was waiting. "Thomas, you are safe."

"I am safe, Gertrude."

"Were you successful?"

"We have recovered the Apostle's bones." Pettigrew managed a tight smile. "Miss Jones proved to be a remarkable magician."

Flinders nodded. "Indeed so."

"And the Veiled One?" Gertrude asked.

"We shot him, but he escaped." He shook his head in disappointment. "He will most certainly be back. Gertrude . . ." He lowered his voice. "The river was full of *bodies*. Heads floated on the river before us. I have never seen anything like that before, and I hope to never see anything like that again."

"I know. The staff told me." Gertrude frowned. "It started two days ago. Something terrible is happening upriver."

"Can you find out?" Flinders asked.

"The way is blocked. Our agents cannot get in—Cossack patrols intercept everyone."

She looked at the floor, and then stared into Flinders's eyes. "This is much bigger than we imagined. I fear the worst."

The small room was silent. Soft footsteps padded outside its closed door. Flinders watched as Pettigrew and Gazelda shuffled uneasily. An electric light buzzed in the ceiling.

Gazelda looked around. "We are missing someone."

"Where is Kudret?"

"He is dead," Flinders told her.

Gertrude covered her eyes. Flinders thought he heard a soft sob. "We were together so many years." She looked up. "You do not know what we did in those years." Tears streamed down her cheeks. "No one will ever know." She straightened up. "His children are safe. I will see that they are returned home."

She covered her face again. "Kudret, Kudret, where have you gone?" Then she composed herself. "I am sorry for that. I am tired. Pay no attention. That was improper of me."

Always the stiff upper lip.

There was another moment of silence, and then Gertrude said, "You must leave now."

She pushed them toward a door. "The car is waiting. It will take you to Latakia. You will have to cross the Syrian desert. The trip will be several days—I've packed the car with food and gasoline in anticipation." Her eyes sought Pettigrew's. "Thomas, be careful. The desert is alive with troops."

"I will."

She smiled. "And Thomas, this time, don't forget to write."

"I will write as soon as we reach London." Pettigrew paused. "But where will you be?"

"I will stay. Baghdad is my home." Her green eyes flashed. "Besides, someone needs to report on what is happening here."

"Now I will worry about your safety."

"How kind of you."

Their eyes met. Their hands touched briefly, and then they stood apart.

"Goodbye."

"Goodbye."

Words are not enough.

As the car drove off, Flinders looked back. Bright light outlined Gertrude's figure in the open door. She waved, and then the door closed, and the night became black.

☜

The car hit a bump, and Flinders returned to the night desert. He sighed and settled back in his seat to get some sleep. But sleep did not easily come to him; a figure in red danced behind his closed eyes.

The desert opened before him, barren and pitiless.

SIX

Whither Do You March?

T he night was cold. The seats were hard. The car bounced. His neck hurt. Fitful sleep finally came to him. And then the sun slid over the horizon. Opal light spread across the plain. Black rocks cast long shadows in the purple light of dawn. A breeze whistled in his ear.

At first, he could see nothing in the morning haze. Then the sun rose higher, an opal in the mist, and gradually dark shapes appeared. Flinders sat up and peered through the grimy windscreen.

"My God! Those are people."

The car stopped at the edge of the low hill; the desert floor opened below. The mist evaporated and the plain became clear. Flinders stared. A line of marchers stretched as far as his eye could see. He shook his head in disbelief. A dark ribbon of despair wound its way across the bright gray and brown sand and merged with the horizon. The ribbon left a trail of bundles and clothes as it moved.

He turned. "Thomas, there are thousands upon thousands!"

Pettigrew got out and walked to the precipice. "Flinders, this is unimaginable. Gazelda, stay where you are!"

The desert groaned with crying voices. Echoing winds carried the terrible sound. Dark shapes moved in the bright sand. Some walked and cried; others walked in silence, their heads bowed. Clouds of fitful dust swirled around the sad figures. Horsemen spurted clumps of sand as they rode up and down the line.

"What is this?" Flinders asked the driver. "I do not believe what I see."

"Death march," the driver replied.

"Who are they?"

"Armini, Ashuri, Greeks, all mix."

"There are no young men."

"Dead. Throw into wells."

"Where are they going?"

"Nowhere, effendi."

"They go south. Is there anything there?"

"Desert, effendi."

"What can we do?'

"Nothing."

"Why not?"

"Already dead, effendi."

"Steer the car along the line." Pettigrew's voice shook. "They go south, and we go north. At some point, we will have to cross through them."

"I cannot watch," Gazelda said. She covered her eyes.

The car moved slowly forward. The line wavered and moved. Solitary figures slumped and fell as they watched. Occasional small shapes lay in the dust as the car passed.

"Those are children."

"Children not live in desert, effendi."

Faces turned to watch as the crawling car slid past the walkers. Heads turned and hands stretched out.

"They are reaching out to us," Gazelda sobbed. "They want water. We must stop. Could we give them some water?"

Pettigrew frowned at her. "Do you wish to play God and decide who shall have water and who shall not?" He turned to the driver. "Drive on."

"Yes, effendi."

The line of anguish passed slowly by.

"Driver, stop!" Pettigrew said.

Brakes squealed and dust flew; the car plowed sideways in the sand. A woman staggered out of the line and stood in front of the car. Her eyes were empty, and her cheeks were sunken in. Her long dress was torn. She held out a blanketed figure.

"Armini," the driver said.

"She holds a child."

Pettigrew frowned. "That blanket is too stiff. There is something wrong." He got out. "I am a physician. I must help."

The woman pushed her child at Pettigrew. He unrolled the blanket from its head. His face tightened. "It is a girl about five years old, and she has been dead for some time." He shook his head. "The mother has carried a dead child for days." He pulled at the blanket.

The woman held the child tighter.

Pettigrew shook his head. "She will not let her daughter go."

"No, effendi."

"Is there nothing you can do?" Gazelda asked.

"Nothing, effendi. Child dead, mother dead, all dead."

Pettigrew got back in the car. His jaw was clenched, and his eyes were half shut. "I am a physician, but I cannot help." Then he whispered softly to himself. "I cannot help here any more than I could help in Cairo."

Flinders stared at the endless line of people. *Walking, walking. Walking to nowhere.* To Rome, to the desert, to nowhere—it is all the same. *The two trudged through the dust. Smiling Roman soldiers lounged in doorways. A helmeted officer, his plumes blowing white, saluted them with a flagon of wine. Finally, Peter spoke to the silent figure beside him.*

"Whither do you march?"

The figure replied, "I march to Rome to be crucified."

Peter replied, "Then I shall come with you."

But we cannot march with you.

Flinders looked back. The car slowly moved on, a snake's tail of dust marking its passage. The woman stood in the sand. Her still figure grew smaller as the car moved away. Finally, he could see only a cloud of ochre dust.

The line of marchers crawled by.

Finally, Pettigrew pointed. "Driver, there is a gap in the line. Drive through it."

The car turned; its tires skidded on an abandoned bedroll.

They leave their existence in the sand. A rich life, a full life.

The village quieted for the night, the smell of cooking lamb entertaining the taste buds. Children laughed and their mothers called them to dinner. Men relaxed after a hard day in the fields. Perhaps a glass of wine to settle the stomach. They begin to doze; dishes clattered and women sang softly in the kitchen. The sound was music to their ears as they drifted off, and the children slipped into sleep. The women smiled and covered them with warm blankets. And life was good; the morning would be bright, and the fields would shine like silver in the sun.

But tomorrow would never happen. Men with rifles and hard eyes would kick down the doors.

Like the legions of centuries before.

The car drove on in the heat. Its engine smelled of hot oil and the sun blazed bright above it.

"Stop the car!" Flinders stood up from his seat. "Look at that." He pointed to a woman facedown in the sand. Two small figures pulled at her lifeless body.

"Ashuri."

"Enough is enough!" Flinders vaulted out of the car and ran to the body. Pettigrew followed and knelt to examine the woman.

Her face was covered in sand.

"She's been dead for at least a day." Pettigrew looked up. "Another one. How many are there?"

Flinders reached for the children. "But these are still alive."

They were light in Flinders's arms. Their faces were streaked with dirt, their eyes too big for their heads. "I feel nothing but bare bones," he said. "It is like they have no flesh. Their arms and legs are like sticks. What men have done this to you?" Flinders walked slowly, holding the two children, a boy and a girl. Both sobbed in terror.

"Behind you, Flinders!" Pettigrew shouted.

Flinders turned and looked.

Horsemen thundered at them.

"Cossacks," the driver warned. "They will kill us!"

Assyrians staggered in all directions. Horsemen rode them down and slashed at them with sabers. A Cossack swerved and charged Flinders. Flinders pushed the children behind him and drew his pistol. The Cossack's saber sliced down as he leaned forward to deliver the cut. Flinders stepped back and fell; the children sprawled on either side of him.

"Thomas, throw me a saber; this damn pistol doesn't work!" The moment in time it took for Pettigrew to throw the sword felt like an eternity. He caught it in his hands, jumped to his feet, and charged the horseman.

"Now, you coward, you meet Cyrano himself." *Plumes fluttered over his broad hat; the blade sang in his hand.* "I dash my hat and draw my sword with slashing air. Come to me, good sir, come to me if you dare."

The Cossack swung again. Flinders charged again and swung his blade. "You are overmatched," he cried, "my Russian friend! You face a swordsman beyond compare."

Sabers clanged as Flinders's sword blocked a blow. He half fell to his knee and then rose and drove the blade forward. "I thrust home— now die if you dare." The Cossack fell; his horse continued running. Flinders stepped over the Cossack and thrust his blade twice into the man's chest.

"And *that* is for threatening my children!" Flinders dusted himself off. "Thank you very much, Thomas." He breathed heavily. "Thomas, I think Cyrano needs to retire."

He dropped the saber.

"Cyrano will never retire," Pettigrew said.

Flinders ran back to the children. "Now, what shall we do with these?"

Pettigrew went to the car and opened the door. "Hurry, the Cossacks are regrouping."

"I know," Flinders said and then gathered the children in his arms and hugged them tightly. "These little birds are coming with me. You are all right now."

"They are starving." Pettigrew looked concerned. "Flinders, they may not survive. They need to be in a hospital."

"Thomas, they will survive."

Pettigrew shook his head.

"I will it."

"Flinders, please . . ." Gazelda whispered. "Do you understand?"

Flinders cracked. "I will it!"

Pettigrew looked at him. "Let me see what I can do." He felt their pulses. "Gazelda, do you have some water? They are badly dehydrated."

"They are mine, Thomas."

"I understand, my friend," Pettigrew said.

Flinders hugged the dark heads. *You must survive.* He growled; the rumble reverberated deep in his chest. "I will breathe my strength into you, and you will survive."

They eased the children into the car. The boy sat on Flinders's lap; the girl sat on Gazelda's. Flinders looked at Pettigrew. "Give them some water."

Pettigrew shook his head. "I doubt they will last the night. We were too late."

Gazelda held the girl. Tears fell on her head.

"We are not too late." Flinders stroked the boy's head. "Stay with me, little birds."

Someone knocked on the door. He got up and opened it.

A policeman stood on the step. "Mr. Petrie?"

"Constable McDonald, what brings you here?"

"Stay with me, little birds. Stay with me. This will never happen again."

"Driver, let's get out of here." Pettigrew slammed the car door behind him. "The Cossacks are coming this way."

"There are too many of them," the driver said.

Wheels spun and the car darted forward. Flinders turned back to watch. The line of despair faded into the brown of the desert as the car drove on. After a few moments, there was nothing but a cloud of dust stretching along the desert floor. *They have disappeared as though they never were.* He pulled the children closer. Three dark heads huddled together in its back seat. *But you have not disappeared.* Night fell, covering everything with a cloak of blackness. The desert waited, dark in its history, bright in its hope.

The night was long. Flinders slept in spurts. Then his eyes opened, and he rubbed them. The dark sky was growing brighter in anticipation of the dawn. The children breathed next to him. *Men die when the clock strikes four and life is at its lowest ebb. But we are still alive, and the sun rises at last.*

He snuggled the dark heads. *You live; I hear your breath. I hear your heartbeat.*

He drew a long breath. "The sun rises, and so do you." *I must give you names.*

He nudged Gazelda. "What should we name these little birds?"

Gazelda shook herself awake. "I do not know," she said heavily. "They have no names."

"They have names. We just do not know them." Flinders thought a moment. "But I will give them names now. The girl will be Maryam, after another woman with gray eyes who danced in my mind. The boy will be Benyamin, after the house of the Patriarch." Flinders paused. "We can give them new names, but in the dark of the night they will remember the old ones. The ones their mother held them to and sang at bedtime. The ones their father laughed and called out in the morning. The ones that were destroyed in the desert."

But their old names will never be destroyed; they will never be forgotten.

Flinders looked at Pettigrew. "Thomas, I grow old."

"You do not grow old, my friend. You just grow wise."

The blue lights drove relentlessly through the desert. As the light brightened, Flinders saw only empty expanse, but he sensed that a thousand unseen eyes were watching him. Green lizards peered at the car through obsidian eyes and then disappeared. Other creatures remained invisible. His mind's eye watched a desert leopard yawn in the rising sun and then curl up for a nap before the morning's hunt.

A pillar of birds took flight, frightened by some unseen menace.

The acrid fragrance of parched plants, wet from the dew of the night, caressed his senses. *I wonder if I shall ever smell the desert again.* Dark turned to light, and a streak of white spread across the solid horizon, splitting the world into sky and land. Dark shapes began to emerge; black figures turned into green plants. Flinders saw distant tents etched against an ever-brightened desert.

"Bedouins, like before," said Pettigrew.

"I hope they are friendly," said Flinders.

A crowd of men and women surrounded the car as it slid to a stop. He had watched as men's fingers uneasily touched rifle triggers. For a moment, no one had moved. Then a tent flap opened, and a familiar figure stepped out. "Ah, detectives Petrie and Pettigrew, you have returned. Ahlan, Ahlan wa Sahlan. Welcome, welcome. Our house is your house." The shaykh looked older; his hair was streaked with gray. "You must stay with us; we have much to talk about and much to remember."

Flinders pointed to the children. "We need your help."

The shaykh gestured and said something in Arabic. Women smiled and reached into the car. They chattered among themselves and carried Maryam and Benyamin to a tent. "Do not worry," the shaykh said. "They will take good care of your children. It is late. We will show you to your beds."

✦

The following morning, Flinders and Pettigrew walked to where the camels were tied. Pettigrew looked over the rope. "I once mounted one of these." He smiled in remembrance. "I thought I would fall and break every bone in my body."

"But you didn't."

"I miss Nelly." Pettigrew sighed. "I wonder what happened to her."

"I can tell you." Flinders smiled. "I had a long talk with the shaykh last night. He said that she was covered with bites, which turned into scars. No one was permitted to ride her ever again. She was cared for and lived long."

"Good."

"The boy who was not sick tended her. He would not let anyone else touch her. His name was Adl, I believe."

Pettigrew smiled. "His mother was quite worried about him."

The shaykh opened the tent flap and beckoned them in. The tent was dark and cool; bright sunlight from the desert outside streamed under its edges. They folded their legs and sat on ottomans. Flinders heard a rhythmic pounding and smelled fresh coffee beans. The rhythm lulled him half asleep.

He did not stay in that state for long—a polite cough brought him back to the dinner. The shaykh smiled. Women placed trays on the low table. *"Take food with your right hand, and do not overreach,"* Lawrence's *voice whispered in his ear.* A young boy, perhaps eight years old, poured the coffee. Flinders stared at him. He had blue eyes and wore a gray gallabiyah.

The shaykh lifted his cup ceremoniously and took a sip. "To see that it is good," he said solemnly. He turned to Flinders. "And now for you. We will drink three cups—one cup for your soul, one cup for your sword, and the last cup because you are my guests."

The coffee was strong and bitter.

The shaykh pointed to a tall man who stood by the tent's flap. "That is Adl. Doctor Pettigrew, you once examined him when he could not water the camels." The shaykh laughed. "He was small then, but now he is our strongest man." The shaykh gestured. "Ya, Adl, come over here. He never forgot you. He helped you up after you fought the Bulbul. He will be my successor. Adl, meet Doctor Pettigrew. He saw you as a boy."

Adl shook Pettigrew's hand.

"I see you have recovered."

The young man smiled and nodded.

"Adl, show Doctor Pettigrew the size of your arm."

The young man flexed his arm.

"He is strong," the shaykh said. Then he waved at the blue-eyed boy. "This is the son of my daughter. There are no other sons, only daughters. He is the best rider of all the boys. He defeats everybody in wrestling. He is tall for his age; his father must have been a tall man. Someday, he too will become the leader of this tribe."

Pettigrew smiled at the boy.

He sees the same eyes.

The shaykh snapped his fingers. "Ya, Omar, come here."

"His name is Omar?"

"Yes. His mother named him after the great Warrior Caliph." The shaykh smiled. "She said his father was a giant of a man with eyes like the blue sky on a clear morning and hair the color of lemons in the sun."

Lawrence once described Pettigrew as Omar.

With hair the color of lemons in the sun.

Thomas, Thomas . . .

Pettigrew and the boy shook hands. Their blue eyes met. Pettigrew pointed to a dagger on the boy's belt. He turned to the shaykh. "That is a very big dagger for such a young boy."

"He always carries it with him."

"Please ask him about the dagger. Where did he get it?"

The shaykh spoke to him in their language and listened as the boy replied.

"He says that his mother gave it to him," the shaykh said, "and that he has always carried it."

"Did she tell him anything about it?"

"She said it was given to her by someone she loved."

"Did she describe that person?"

"No."

"Who was his mother?"

Thomas, you know who his mother was.

"Unayza." The shaykh fingered his prayer beads. "She was my favorite daughter. As a girl, she laughed and played in the sun. Then she grew to be a beautiful woman. I loved her very much." He wiped a tear. "But something happened. She changed. The girl with the braids became someone I could not protect. Then she married my brother. But my brother was not the boy's father."

Unayza said she carried Pettigrew's child.

The shaykh fumbled with his beads and mumbled to himself. "My little Unayza, I tried to save you." He covered his face. "I tried, but I was only a man." He put the beads down.

"Who was his father?"

Thomas, you know who his father is.

"No one knows," the boy spoke in English, which surprised Flinders. "My mother would not say."

"He speaks English."

"I taught him." The shaykh smiled.

Pettigrew looked at the boy. "Omar, does your blade have a notch near the point?"

The boy pulled the blade out and nodded.

"Does it have two stars on the handle?"

Another nod.

"Does it have an inscription?"

The boy examined the blade and nodded again.

"Does the inscription say, 'Let the sword decide'?"

The boy looked up, his eyes wide. "How do you know all this, Doctor Pettigrew?"

"It is a long story," Pettigrew said. "I knew your father, long ago."

Flinders swallowed. *A very long story, indeed.*

Pettigrew turned to face the shaykh. "Where is his mother now?"

"A sad question, Doctor Pettigrew. She died years ago. The Veiled One came down on us. We fought him off. Many were killed, including

Unayza. But before she died, she made her son swear to honor and protect his father. She said that he would know him when he met him."

"Could you tell me more?"

The boy smiled at the memory. "My father was a great warrior.
When he laughed, the desert trembled. When he smiled, the sun hid
itself in envy."

Pettigrew smiled. "A mighty man, indeed."

The boy's eyes flashed. "One day, my father mounted his camel and
rode off to fight the evil jinn. The women wailed until the dunes shook
with the sound."

I remember the sound, thought Flinders, *and so does Thomas.*

The boy pulled the dagger from its sheath. "They fought for days.
Their blows were like hammers ringing in the sky. The sand where they
fought was torn in all directions. Rocks were thrown about, and small
bushes were uprooted."

Pettigrew smiled, rubbing his shoulder. "The battle must have been
terrible to behold."

The boy waved the dagger. "The jinn gave my father a mighty blow.
My father's camel sank to the ground. But they arose, and my father
smote the jinn."

Pettigrew whispered to Flinders. "Now how would he know that?"

"He knows."

I think that you are closer than you imagine.

The boy continued. "Then my father came out of the desert. He
spoke to the tribesmen. 'I have killed the jinn. You are now safe.' The
women cried in happiness. Then he kissed my mother and said, 'I
love you very much. I must go to fight more jinn, but I shall return.'
My mother cried." The boy sighed. "And he rode again into the desert. My mother watched the dust of his tracks until he disappeared
into the dawn."

"He rode off into the dawn?" Pettigrew looked at the carpet.

"Yes, Doctor Pettigrew."

He rode off into the dawn; the car left a trail of dust in the desert.

The shaykh bowed his head. The tent was silent.

The boy smiled. "Someday, my father will return. He will let me hold his great sword. He will show me his scars and tell me his tales. He will hug me, and we will laugh and cry together."

Pettigrew leaned forward. "Your father and I were great friends. Your father loved your mother very much." Pettigrew's eyes moistened.

Thomas, you must tell him the truth.

The shaykh spoke, and the boy listened.

The boy's eyes glistened with delight. "My father comes to me in my dreams."

"In your dreams?"

"Yes. When the stars come out, he comes to me."

Pettigrew sighed. "And does he talk to you?"

"Yes." The boy laughed. "He always talks to me." He waved the dagger. "I will wear this dagger to the end of my life. I will make my father proud. I will be his great son, and when he is old, I will comfort him."

Thomas, he is your son. Take him in your arms.

"May I hold the dagger?"

"Yes, but be careful—I have polished it for my father."

Pettigrew carefully turned the dagger in his hands. "It is very sharp."

"Yes, when my father first fought the jinn, he received a blow on this blade. He was sorely wounded."

"Wounded?"

"My mother attended him, and then he arose and went forth."

Every day she sat by his bed.

"The desert trembled at his wrath."

Pettigrew handed the dagger back. "It is very bright."

The boy smiled. "When it sees the light, its brightness is like the sun. Only my father could look at it and not be blinded."

"Yes, when it sees the light."

Thomas once waved the dagger in the sun. Its blade was blinding. He said, "This is a hard blade for a hard people."

"Omar, do you recognize me?"

Now that was a strange question, thought Flinders. *They have only just met.*

"I am not sure. But I think so—you look like someone I know."

"But you have never seen me before?"

"Your eyes are like my father's."

They are mirror images of each other.

"How could you know that?"

"God wills all things, Abul hol," the shaykh murmured from where he sat.

They chanted, 'ya, ya, Abul hol,' as Thomas rode out. Indeed, God wills all things, great and small.

The prayers were long; the dinner was short. Neither Flinders nor Pettigrew spoke much. Gazelda watched in wide-eyed silence. Pettigrew never took his eyes off the boy.

And then it was over.

As they left the tent, Flinders put his arm around Pettigrew's shoulder. "We grow old, my friend, and our past catches up with us."

"Our past catches up with us," Pettigrew repeated, wiping the tears that now streamed from his face. "Flinders, I abandoned his mother—I cannot destroy his dream." He straightened up. "Flinders, I could not tell him that his father was an aging Englishman in a frumpy suit. I could not do that."

"But you *are* his father," Flinders said. "You *are* the mighty warrior of his dreams, and you *have* given him those dreams. No father could do more for a son."

Pettigrew sighed. "You once said that we should not destroy the legend of Cleopatra. That she should not be reduced to a shriveled mummy in some museum. I cannot destroy a legend that my son lives for. He lives for a great hero. I am not that hero."

"But you *are* that hero," Flinders pleaded. "Thomas, you have been my friend for thirty years. You cannot do this."

"Flinders, remember the saying about the mills of the gods, that they grind 'exceedingly fine'?"

"They do, my friend, they do."

"If I tell him, he will want to come with me. I cannot take him to London. There he will be a fish out of water. People will see him as the odd bedouin boy." He covered his face with his hands. "No, he belongs here. This is his world. Someday, he will lead the tribe. He will live surrounded by friends and be secure in his person."

"You are giving up your son."

"Flinders, we cannot change our worlds no matter how much we want to. I am his father, and a father must protect his son. I cannot destroy his dream."

Pettigrew shrugged and disappeared into a tent.

"But you can destroy our own dream," Flinders said quietly.

॰ᜰ᠔

The night was still soft as he escorted Gazelda to her tent. A crescent moon glowed pale in the shimmering sky. Gazelda looked up at the shining vault. "It is as though I am standing on the edge of the world. I feel like a shadow figure in a great emptiness of light."

"A shadow figure, yes."

"You are sad," she said softly. "This evening has been very hard for you. Your face was painful to watch, as you saw your friend so badly hurt."

"Yes."

"You need cheering up." She smiled. "Did I ever tell you about the time Holmes and Watson went camping?"

"I believe I have heard that one before—but, do go on."

"They set up their tent in a clearing. Then they went for a walk.

When they came back, the tent was gone. 'Where did it go?' Watson asked. 'Hamlet,' said Holmes. 'Hamlet?' Watson looked confused. Holmes replied, 'To be or not to be, that is the tent.'"

"You made that up. That is not the way it goes."

"I know." She giggled.

He smiled.

He opened the tent flap, and she went in.

"Good night, Gazelda."

"Good night, Flinders."

Flinders walked slowly to the silent car. Flashes of starlight danced off its still shape. He shivered slightly in the desert air. The smell of motor oil mixed with sage and dust; somewhere animals murmured uneasily. He opened the glove box and found a cigar.

"May I join you?" Pettigrew asked, approaching. His voice was tired. "I could not sleep."

They leaned against the car. Gray smoke outlined their figures against the sparkling blackness.

"Do you suppose they are still marching?" Flinders asked.

"The Assyrians, you mean?"

"Yes."

"And the Armenians?"

"Yes."

"They are still marching," Pettigrew said.

"To nowhere?"

"To nowhere."

"I can hear their cries across the desert. The wind carries them like a sigh."

"Their cries will always echo in our ears."

Pettigrew hears the cries of Assyrians. Woolley heard the rumble of Hittite chariots. Is this desert like some vast time machine that forever records everything in its sands? Are all the sounds of centuries lying here, waiting to rise up again like ancient ghosts?

Pettigrew examined his cigar.

"What about the woman with the dead child?" Flinders lit a match.

"We will never know."

"At least I have two little birds."

"So you do."

Pettigrew drew a long breath and looked at his cigar's flickering tip.

Flinders placed his elbows on the hood.

The world of the sword is a cruel world.

"Thomas, in the ancient valley of the Nile sit two gigantic monoliths. They are called the 'Colossi of Memnon.' During the day they are quiet, reposing in their majesty, seated figures that loom above the plain." Flinders lowered his voice. "The sun beats on them during the day and etches them against the glow of sunset in the evening. But at night, when the wind blows cold down that barren valley and dust devils arise, they moan for release from their stony prisons." He shook his head. "Thomas, we are like those monoliths. During the day we bestride the world, but at night we cry for release."

"Maybe so." Pettigrew watched his cigar smoke curl upward across the sky's bright pinpoints.

Red ash glowed and disappeared in the warm night.

"I remember how we smoked once before," Flinders said. "You leaned on the sphinx. I sat on the bench."

"We were younger, then."

Flinders nodded. "Now, we are older."

"Older, but perhaps wiser."

"We have seen too much suffering."

"Too much, indeed." Pettigrew sighed.

Finally, Flinders snuffed his cigar out. "Go to sleep, my friend. The dawn will come all too soon."

He watched Pettigrew slowly walk to his tent. Then he went to his own, but sleep did not come easily to him. The cold wind lifted the edges of the tent and curled around his sleeping figure. He turned uneasily in his blanket. Dim lines of marchers crossed behind his eyes. Once, he woke up, shivering in cold sweat. A woman held a blanketed figure out. He opened the blanket and stared—a skull smiled toothlessly at him.

For Flinders, dawn came all too soon. He stepped out of the tent and stared at the sky. A rainbow of colors stretched across the horizon. Gertrude had once said, "It is like being in the center of an opal." The black tents loomed stark in the foreground. A gentle morning breeze caressed his nose with the smell of cooking. He shivered in the cold morning air.

Gazelda came out of her tent.

"Good morning," Flinders said. "This has not been the fairy castles and handsome princes that you dreamed about."

Sheep bleated somewhere in the encampment.

"I think that it has." She smiled. "Fairy castles and handsome princes are only images of the real thing. It is the reality in the cold dawn that counts."

"And have you met that handsome prince?"

"Indeed, I may have." She glanced shyly up at him. "And have you found the fairy princess?"

"Indeed, I may have."

What am I to do?

Tent flaps opened and women came out and set up small braziers. The camp became alive with the smell of cooking. Children spilled out onto the dust. Animals cried out to be fed. The silence of the dawn ended with the laughter of the day.

Pettigrew stepped out of his tent. "The shaykh asked me to care for his sick people."

"As you did before."

"As we did before."

Pettigrew spent the morning going from tent to tent, tending to the sick. "Once again, I have no bag, Flinders." He sighed. "What kind of a physician has no bag?"

"A very caring one, my friend."

Flinders followed behind him, along with a crowd of women and children. The boy trailed Pettigrew's tall figure. *Just like his mother did so many years ago.* Flinders followed the boy's eyes. They never left Pettigrew. *What does he see? A tall Englishmen with graying hair? Or a giant of a man with hair the color of lemons in the sun?*

The sun beat down as they moved from tent to tent. "There are no babies to hold today, Flinders." Pettigrew grinned. "You will have to amuse yourself some other way."

"Yes, some other way," he replied. But he watched his friend and was saddened. Pettigrew sometimes looked behind him, as though he was searching for someone. Once, he jumped as though he had seen a ghost. When he could no longer bear to watch his friend suffer, Flinders trudged toward his tent. A woman in black stood in front of him; she held Maryam by the hand. She dropped her veil and smiled. Flinders smiled back; she was one of the women who had taken the children away.

A large teddy bear appeared in front of him, blocking the face of the child who held it.

"What have you got there?" Flinders knelt before the child and laughed. "That teddy bear is as big as you are."

The child lowered the bear, and Flinders saw that it was the little girl. Two serious gray eyes regarded him; two small arms held the bear.

"Come along," Flinders said, and held out his hand. A small hand reached out and took it.

Flinders took Maryam and sat down on a dusty camel saddle. She looked at him with wide eyes. "Let me see you." He smiled. "Yes, the ladies of the camp have washed and fed you."

Her gray eyes were very serious.

"Your cheeks seem fuller, and your face is clean."

Flinders pulled out a large comb. "Gazelda gave this to me. She said that it was just right for small girls. Now hold still while I straighten your hair."

The child wiggled.

"That is not the way to do it," Gazelda said, appearing from nowhere.

"She won't hold still."

"Of course not—you're pulling her hair." Gazelda knelt. "Besides, maybe she doesn't like a man who smells of cognac and cigars."

"That is my cologne, and I use it sparingly."

She gently stroked Maryam's hair. "Give me the comb. Now watch—you take her hair and make three strands, like this. And then you weave them together, like this. Now you try it."

Gazelda frowned in disapproval as he attempted to finish the braid.

"As someone once said, you have much to learn." Then she arched an eyebrow. "Perhaps more practice."

The woman never forgets anything.

She finished braiding Maryam's hair. "That's how it should be done."

"With those braids and that blue dress, you look like a bedouin girl."

"What do you think, Flinders. Should we leave her here?"

"Never," Flinders growled.

"I see." Gazelda's eyes softened.

"She is still much too thin."

Gazelda stood, picked up Maryam, and placed her on her hip. "You need some goat's milk and yogurt. Benyamin is already having lunch."

"Here, you hold this," she said and shoved the bear at Flinders.

She turned and walked toward a tent. "The women of the camp have taken quite a fancy to him." She looked over her shoulder and laughed. "Much like the Englishman who saved his life." A couple of goats followed her; chickens pecked at the sand behind them.

Flinders watched them go. The bear's button eyes stared at him.

There was another bear, once.

The policeman stood in the doorway, his helmet in the crook of his arm.

"There's been an accident, sir."

"Oh?"

"It's your wife and daughter, sir."

"Are they all right?"

"I'm afraid not, sir."

"But that was so long ago," Flinders said aloud. He rubbed his eyes.

"Are you coming?" Gazelda asked.

"In a minute."

What would have happened if I had been driving?

But I cannot live with old memories forever.

"Hurry up. We're waiting."

Flinders got up. The bear smiled at him. *Maybe it is time for another bear.* He put the bear under his arm. *And maybe it is time for another smile.*

He followed them.

I must think about this. It has been so long, and the loss was so heavy. Can I risk those feelings again? The horizons beyond the horizon are far safer.

The chickens scattered and clucked as he passed.

⟲ℰ⟳

The day wore on. Pettigrew walked among the tents. Flinders and Gazelda watched. Women bustled and chattered, and men laughed and fed their flocks. Horses coughed and sheep bleated. Shadows of men and animals rippled between the black tents. The desert breeze strengthened and blew motes of dust.

Then the sun set in a blaze of color. Flinders watched its red haze dissolve behind the line of the horizon. The sky darkened; stars came out and glowed white in the distance. A dark line stretched before his eyes.

Horizons beyond the horizon. What does that mean?

"You look tired." Gazelda's voice was soft in his ear.

"I *am* tired."

"Shall I tell you about the time Holmes disguised himself as a camellia bush?"

"Holmes did no such thing, and you know it."

"How do you know?"

"I have it on the highest authority." Flinders produced a knowing look.

"Highest authority?"

"The horse's mouth, so to speak."

"Indeed, and who would that horse be?"

Flinders's voice dropped to a whisper. "Holmes himself."

"So?"

"Holmes told me that he would never disguise himself as a camellia. He said that he always preferred rose bushes."

Gazelda giggled. "There may be hope for you."

We make insane jokes in an insane world, Flinders thought.

But I am tired. I want to be a boy again and listen to my mother read nursery rhymes.

Then a voice spoke in his head.

"We are tired too. What will you do about us?" The line of marchers drifted behind his eyes. *"You cannot escape us."*

I do not know. I am only a man. I cannot save the world.

"You must try."

I must go—the shaykh awaits. The evening prayers must be recited.

"Come on, Gazelda, let's go to dinner—the couscous smells good."

Dinner was short. The tent was crowded, and the prayers quietly spoken. Pettigrew and the shaykh sat next to each other, brothers in sad memories. The boy served coffee. *As his mother once did.* His blue eyes always watched Pettigrew.

He knows.

He serves coffee to the man with hair the color of lemons in the sun.
Pettigrew sits and watches. He knows as well.
The dinner ends, and now we must leave.
Do we leave this world, or does it leave us?

᧞

Flinders stretched in the morning air. The sun smiled above him, pink turning to white in the sky. The car's engine growled. Flinders and Gazelda put the children in the back seat and climbed in on either side. Pettigrew waited for a moment as though looking for someone, and then sat beside the driver. The car started with a jolt and rolled past the black tents and into the desert.

"And he rode into the desert."

Flinders looked back. A crowd of women in black and men in gray waved goodbye. Rifles fired puffs of smoke into the air as the figures receded into the haze. Trackless desert loomed before the car as it sped through the dust. Gertrude had once said, "The desert has no footpaths." He wondered if she was just talking about a desert.

Flinders turned again for a last look. The figures in black and gray dwindled to nothingness. He thought he saw the flash of a blade in the sun. He was not sure whether Pettigrew saw it as well.

᧞

The drive to Latakia was long and bumpy. Flinders dozed, and the children slept. Dust covered his face; sweat poured down his neck. When he awoke, he saw small tornados of dust whirling before him in the plain. *The desert dances in the sunset before me. Is it a sign of hope?* The heat lessened, and the sky slowly turned to buttermilk and then to gray. A twinkle of lights along the darkening horizon caught his eye.

Latakia or a mirage?

Was all this a dream? Would he wake up in the flat, where the sun shines through the white curtains? Would Elise ring the breakfast bell? Would they go into the dining room and eat muffins and jam?

The steamer's blast shattered the air. Gangways were pulled up; lines were cast off. The skyline of Latakia slid past as the ship put to sea. Gulls circled in its wake. Baggagemen pulled carts along the decks, and passengers disappeared into their cabins. The harbor faded into the distance, and open water lined the horizon. Flinders leaned over the rail and watched the foam pass along the ship's side.

There was a time long ago when I would walk these decks and the ladies in deck chairs would smile and wave their fans. The aunts would frown. I would bow and tip my hat. My world was young and full of hope. But no longer. I have seen too much destruction. Kudret said that his world was vanishing. It may be that my world is vanishing also.

A desert hawk screamed over his head. Flinders looked up at the black speck high in the bright sky. "You are too far out to sea, my friend. You will die if you keep searching these empty waves."

Maybe we are all too far out to sea.

A steward touched his arm. "I have a note from Miss Jones. She wishes to see you." The steward bowed. "She is in cabin one-oh-four, sir." The steward pointed. "It's just down that corridor."

She wishes to see me.

Flinders walked down the corridor. It seemed endless, an empty line of closed doors and meaningless numbers. *Ah, cabin number 104.* Flinders opened the door and stopped. The knob was still tight in his hand. *Do I dare go in?*

He turned the knob.

"Miss Jones," he said, and a vision in white smiled back. "You astonish me."

"My name is Gazelda, remember?"

"Indeed, I do, Gazelda."

He closed the cabin door.

SEVEN

To Dance a Tango

They took a cab to the station. Pettigrew sat beside the driver; Flinders and Gazelda shared the back seat. Both sat in silence during the long cab ride to the station. Gazelda took off her glasses and rubbed her eyes. She stifled a few sniffles. Flinders stared out the window. Their hands touched accidentally several times on the seat between them. When the cab reached the station, Flinders got out and unloaded her luggage. A porter took it. Flinders walked her to the train. No one spoke. They stopped on the platform.

Flinders shook her hand and smiled. "It's been fun. Thank you."

A small bird cannot stay in the hand of a condemned man, and neither can you.

"Yes, it's been fun."

"Say hello to Divinius."

"I will."

Their eyes met and held for a long moment.

Then she said, "I have been in love with you ever since the moment I saw you in the stacks at the Ashmolean." She grasped his hand. "But then you acted as though I didn't exist." She smiled. "When the Veiled One was about to kill you, and you looked at me, I had to save you." She sighed. "I couldn't let you go." She lowered her eyes. "And then you came to me." She turned and fled up the short stairs. "Goodbye." Her voice carried across the platform.

She opened the carriage door and disappeared.

Flinders watched her go.

I will miss you. I love you too.

The train chugged off. Flinders watched it glide down the shining rails until it became a speck on the horizon. He sighed and climbed back into the cab.

"It's time to go home, Thomas," he said.

☙

Baker Street was empty in the evening sun. The brown buildings lining it turned pale pink in the fading light.

"This is the first time that we have come home and it's not raining," Flinders said. He got out of the cab and looked at the sky. "It's still sunny."

The cab drove off. Flinders and Pettigrew picked up their valises and climbed the front steps. Flinders took a last look at the sky. "But not for long, I see rain clouds."

The door opened, and Elise stepped out. "Thank heavens that you are back. I was so worried." She put her hands to her face and then rubbed them on her white apron. "Come in, come in! Leave your luggage in the hall." They went up the narrow stairs. Framed photographs of themselves as younger men flowed past. They entered the dining room. The puffy birds still circled endlessly. The decanter with the Medusa stopper still sat on the hunt bar. Nothing had changed.

"Where did those tulips come from?" Pettigrew asked.

"I cabled Elise to buy some for our return," Flinders replied. "To remember someone."

"Yes, to remember," Pettigrew said. "They are red."

"Red is for the heart."

"Yes, for the heart."

"I see there is also a bottle of raki on the hunt bar."

"I made a promise."

Pettigrew nodded.

"Now, we are home," Flinders said. *But will we ever be home?*

"I see the decanter has been refilled," Pettigrew said. "I'll be back in a moment. I need to unpack something. Pour some cognac."

Flinders went to the window and stared out. "Why do I always look out these windows?" The street was almost empty. He saw a man hurrying below, bending forward against the splatter of beginning raindrops. He held his hat tight with one hand and pulled his raincoat close around his neck with the other. "Why do we always hurry through life?" he said aloud, though the room was empty. Then Flinders thought he saw something else. *The yellow eyes glow. The tiger glides toward me. I cannot move. I can see it in my mind, but I cannot see it with my eyes.*

He turned away and studied the portrait on the wall. Two men in suits, holding bowlers, stared back with dark, unwinking eyes. "We were young and solemn once. Now we are no longer young." He laughed. "But we are still solemn. Too solemn, I think."

Someday, years from now, a stranger will look at that portrait and ask, "Who were these men?"

He leaned into the hall. The golden tiger gleamed on the floor; Sarah Bernhardt smiled from the wall.

Everything is quiet here. The cries of the marchers are silent here. The world of the sword does not exist here.

He went back into the dining room and waited.

"Hurry, Thomas," he called. "I feel a song coming on."

The white curtains slowly turned dark.

"I was right." Flinders laughed. "It is going to be a dark and stormy night." He poured two glasses of cognac and picked up one. Medusa stared from its stem. "I wonder if she is glad to see us." He held the glass to the light. "I wonder if anybody is glad to see us." His eyes became lost in the amber liquid and his mind's silent eye opened.

They are gone: Mariam and Kudret and all the rest, vanished into the desert of time.

No one will remember Mariam's smile. "I am an Assyrian. Do you like what you see?"

But I will remember.

Or Kudret's look when he said, "This old kocek has one more dance left"?

Yes, I will remember.

Or the eyes of the woman in the moonlight, surrounded by her dead children?

I will always remember.

But who else will remember? What will happen to those memories when I am gone? In time, the portrait will be sold and end up in a dusty shop in Soho along with other forgotten antiques. And when that stranger stares into our dark eyes in that dusty shop in Soho, maybe he will ask, "What did those dark eyes see?" But that stranger will never know what wonderful and terrible things those dark eyes have seen.

"I need another drink," Flinders said, sighing.

Pettigrew returned and handed him a letter. "Gazelda made me promise to give you this when we got home."

Flinders opened it and read:

Dear Flinders,

I enjoyed working with you. I earnestly hope that we can work together again. You are a great detective.

I will miss you.

—G. Jones

He put the letter down; the blue eyes and big smile danced across his mind. *I will miss you too. Very, very much.* He went to the window and looked out. *Where have you gone? You grew on me softly until I knew your every smile, your every laugh. You became a part of my existence.* He spread the curtains. Rain swept across the street below. A red bus passed below. Its upper deck was empty, and the wooden seats glistened wet with rain.

My life has become like that bus, going nowhere and empty.

A car horn honked.

Flinders looked down at the street. A young woman, her head covered by an umbrella, was getting into a car. She could not fold the umbrella. The driver, a young man, jumped out of the car and helped her. They laughed and hugged; rain beat on them, but they did not seem to care. "All the rain in the world could pour down on them, but it wouldn't matter as long as they had each other. Perhaps, just perhaps, the Dutchman could find a hug in the rain."

His eyes clouded.

She would smile and make up outrageous jokes. What was the last one?

Ah, yes. I remember. It was raining; water dripped off our umbrellas. "You are sad, and you need cheering up. I will tell you a joke," she said. Her eyes flashed at me. "One morning, Holmes got ready to go to Scotland Yard. 'Watson,' he said. 'Be sure to watch the front door. Never take your eyes off it. Moriarty may try to break in.' Watson replied, 'I will never let it out of my sight.' Holmes went to Scotland Yard. After a while, Watson showed up. 'Watson, why are you here? I told you never to take your eyes off the front door,' Holmes said. 'I haven't,' Watson smiled. 'I have brought it with me.'"

He smiled at the memory.

Such audacious nonsense.

She has become the Scheherazade of old Holmes jokes. She has become my Scheherazade.

We stood outside the basilica. The sky was dark, and the wind blew our umbrellas. We had just handed the emissary the Apostle's casket. The priest

had thanked us and said, "You have rendered a great service to our peo-
ple. We will return the relic to its place of honor in Erbil." Then he smiled.
"The Patriarch said that you were most kind, and that even King Herod
would have been impressed." He shook my hand. "We will take good care
of Maryam and Benyamin."

The nuns took the children through a door.

The room was hot and dry. A steam radiator bubbled and hissed in a
corner, and the bare wood floor smelled of fresh varnish. I watched them
leave. They turned and waved goodbye—two small smiles—and then the
door closed with a thud.

That was the last that I saw of them.

We walked outside and into the rain.

"You have given up your children," Gazelda said.

"I am a middle-aged bachelor; I cannot care for children. They need a
family. My time has passed."

She looked at me and smiled. "Are you so sure about that?"

We got into the car and drove to the station. The wipers thumped softly,
and the seats were damp. I had to tell her. Pettigrew sat in front and pre-
tended that he could not hear. She cried and so did I. Then she was gone,
and the rain drizzled on my head.

Flinders closed the curtains.

But why should I let her go?

"Why, indeed?"

Pettigrew looked up. "You said something?"

"It would be a shame to end such a wonderful collaboration.
We could work together on many other matters." Flinders laughed.
"Now that I think of it, that is an excellent idea." He heard a car
drive off. *They have managed to fold the umbrella.* "I'll send a letter.
I am sure she will be delighted at the prospect." He read the letter
again. "And I will be delighted as well." He turned from the window,
waved Gazelda's letter, and began to whistle "Come, Josephine, in
My Flying Machine."

"You seem suddenly happy," Pettigrew said. He looked surprised.

"I am. Thomas, do you like teddy bears?"

"Teddy bears?" Pettigrew looked puzzled. "Now what are you talking about?"

"A thought that came to me."

Flinders waltzed around the table and put his arms up as though he were dancing with a woman and warbled "Come, Josephine."

Pettigrew laughed. "You have a good voice."

"It was all that training as a choirboy."

"The image boggles my mind." Pettigrew dodged out of Flinders's way. "You seem ready to sing."

"Yes, with relish."

"I am ready as well." Pettigrew raised his glass. "Here's to Fathers Boris and Divinius and the whole singing crew." He looked at Flinders. "Including Gazelda."

"A lovely contralto, I believe." Flinders looked back. "And let us not forget Gertrude."

"Green eyes, I believe."

They broke into a loud chorus of "Flow Gently, Sweet Afton." Pettigrew waved his glass and thundered the words in a heavy bass. Flinders danced a few steps of an Assyrian folk dance and complemented the bass line with a bel canto baritone.

Elise opened the dining room door and stuck her head in. "That is so good to hear." She laughed. "Dinner will be ready soon."

Pettigrew bowed to her, sweeping the room with his arms and grinning ear to ear. Then he caught her and whirled her around the room. She giggled.

I have missed that smile. Now we all smile. It has been so long without a smile in the world of the sword.

Flinders began an Irish step dance, his shoes stamping on the oak floor as he sang. He spun and caught up with Pettigrew and Elise, and the three of them bounced around the dining table. The puffy birds

swirled around the walls. Lightning flashed outside. The curtains fluttered. The flat shook to the melody.

Then the singing slowed to a stop.

They looked at each other.

Flinders picked up his glass and then put it down. "Thomas, I saw
the tiger again," he said.

"You will always see the tiger, my friend."

"What do you mean?"

Pettigrew put his hand on Flinders's shoulder. "The tiger is you."
He refilled his glass. "Remember when we first met in that hall at
Oxford?" Pettigrew stared at his glass.

"Yes, you were watching an ant column climb the wall."

Pettigrew took a sip. "The hall was dark, but I could see its far wall.
I heard soft footsteps coming toward me."

"It was raining," Flinders said. "And I was wearing rubber boots."

"I looked up and thought I saw something. A strange shadow moving down the wall." Pettigrew held his glass to the light.

"I was wearing a slicker and carrying a pack of books on my hip. I
was bent over."

"It was distorted, and I couldn't be sure, but for an instant, I imagined that a tiger was padding toward me." Pettigrew cupped his glass
in both hands.

"Then you came around the corner and I saw a student with dark
eyes and thick black hair. You seemed surprised. You said, 'My name
is Flinders. What's yours?'" Pettigrew continued. "You spoke in a soft
brogue. I said to myself, 'Who is this Irishman?'"

"You never told me."

"That was long ago," Pettigrew said.

"You think I am a tiger?"

Pettigrew swirled his cognac and then put his glass down. "No, you
are not a tiger, but a tiger is within you. We all have our tigers."

Medusa stared at him from the glass's stem. The curtains fluttered slightly; their color alternated between yellow and white as the storm progressed. Flinders saw Pettigrew's face change with the changing light. He looked tired; his drawn features reflected off the polished dining table.

"All of us," Pettigrew added. "Even the Veiled One."

"The Veiled One?" Flinders asked. "Do you think we shall meet him again?"

Pettigrew nodded. "As I said in the palace, rest assured that he will return."

"And then what?"

"And then the tiger will come forth."

"Now you have become a modern-day Sophocles, pondering our tragic flaws."

"I have a passing acquaintance with Sophocles, as I said once before, and you would be one of his most interesting protagonists."

"So be it." Flinders laughed. "Come, let us adjourn to the sitting room and see what the Royal Mail has brought us."

"More love letters, I suppose." The chinoiserie table overflowed. Pettigrew picked up an envelope. "This is from a solicitor, and it is addressed to you."

"Open it, please."

"It says that you have adopted two children, a Benyamin and a Maryam."

Flinders smiled. "Indeed, so. The boy is strong, and the girl has gray eyes."

"How did you do that?"

"Gertrude helped me."

"Ah, Gertrude." Pettigrew smiled to himself. "A woman of many talents and many passions."

Then he looked serious. "But what will you do with them?"

"I have arranged for both of them to go to Chicago. I will support them."

"Chicago?"

"An American city. It has a large Assyrian community, and they will be taken care of there. They will laugh and dance and play in the sun." He smiled. "The girl will take piano lessons in honor of a great musician. Someday she may even be able to play 'Twinkle, Twinkle, Little Star.'"

"I am honored." Pettigrew grinned. "And the boy?"

"The boy will learn to fence, and perhaps to recite poetry."

"Something from the French."

"Indeed, something about a poet with a big nose."

"And will they remember the strange Englishman who came out of the desert and rescued them?"

"Probably not." Flinders sighed. "Probably not."

"Ah, you have become the unknown benefactor, like the character in *Great Expectations*."

"Great expectations, indeed." Flinders nodded. "Yes, they will have great expectations."

I could not save the woman, but I can save the children.

"They will not know who you are," Pettigrew said. "You have given up your children."

"And you have given up your son."

Pettigrew closed his eyes. "One day, my son will lead his people across the desert. He will guide them by following the stars. On clear nights, I can look up at the same stars. We will be together in the starry sky. We will meet under the glittering vault." Pettigrew smiled. "And one day he will come to me and say, 'Father, I have missed you.'"

"He will be tall and strong?"

"Yes, strong and hard like the desert itself."

"And he will greet you?"

"We will hug, and his eyes will be soft."

"Soft like a rose?"

"Yes."

The clock chimed in the dining room. Traffic murmured in the street below. Cleopatra stared down, her face half-hidden in shadow.

"And what will happen with Maryam and Benyamin?"

"One day, I shall go to Chicago to ascertain my children's progress."

"You will listen to the notes of a piano?"

"Yes, and perhaps later there will be a dance."

"A tango, I suspect."

"Fathers do dance with their daughters, you know."

"And Benyamin?"

"We will don the fencer's uniform and make a few passes to see if his wrist is supple enough."

"Indeed," Pettigrew said and smiled. "I am sure that it will be."

The sitting room was silent and empty.

"I need another drink," Pettigrew said.

"Yes, Thomas, and so do I."

"We dream old men's lonely dreams. Of events that may never happen."

"What are we to do?" Flinders asked.

"I do not know."

Flinders frowned. "We wander the world alone, my friend."

Pettigrew nodded. "Like the Dutchman condemned to sail the sea."

"We are condemned as well."

"Yes."

"But we dream."

"Yes, we dream," Pettigrew echoed.

"And sometimes those dreams become reality." Flinders smiled.

"We are like old elephants searching for the elephant graveyard."

"Old elephants can dream, as well."

"Dreams? What are dreams?" Pettigrew's eyes were moist.

"Dreams are the expression of hope."

"Hope?"

"Yes, we have hope," Flinders said. "There is always tomorrow."

"Tomorrow?"

"Trampling about like an elephant is really not my cup of tea, or cognac for that matter." Flinders grinned. "I dance a superb tango and you float like foam on the waves."

"So?"

"The sun will rise; the night will fade." Flinders smiled. "And tomorrow brings another day and another task."

"Now what?"

"The 'what' is that this place needs is a good redecorating." Flinders surveyed the walls, the furniture, the curtains. "And so do we. You have been looking a little frumpy lately. You admitted it yourself."

"I shudder to find out what you have in mind."

"I know an excellent tailor in Saville Row who can bring back the old Pettigrew." Flinders put a finger alongside his nose and pretended to think. "If that Herculean task can be accomplished."

"I don't want to be tailored."

"You didn't want to be a pasha, either. But you became a hero. So there is hope."

Flinders grinned. "My mother used to read me a children's story about a reluctant dragon." He peered at Pettigrew. "Now that I look at you, you are that dragon."

"Nonsense."

"Yes, yes, a great hulking beast in an ill-fitting suit."

"Dragons don't wear suits."

"Details, details, always details. You really have no imagination."

"But I do." Pettigrew smiled. "I see you as an overaged Saint George." He laughed. "You march around the world wildly waving your saber, simpering, and bowing to the ladies."

Flinders laughed. "Thomas, sometimes you astonish me."

Pettigrew's eyes twinkled. "Irish mothers are not the only ones who read children's stories. Now, about that redecorating." Pettigrew scowled. "You're not thinking of doing something outrageous? I remember when you wanted to make the flat into a Roman villa."

"I once thought of using Hadrian's villa as a design guide. A Doric column here, a statue of Caesar there, but I think something more modern is in order."

"More modern? Like what?" Pettigrew frowned. "I shudder at the thought. You're not going to do up the place like some crazy cubist, are you?"

"Now that is an idea." Flinders thought a moment. "Perhaps in the manner of Picasso. But no." He shook his head. "There is an American named Wright who has done wonderful things."

"I've never heard of him."

"He designed a magnificent hotel in Tokyo."

"This is a flat, not a hotel."

Flinders grinned. "This will be so exciting."

Pettigrew frowned.

"There is something else, I think." Flinders pushed Pettigrew into the sitting room. "Look what I had delivered." He pointed to a small mahogany cabinet with a curved lid and a crank on one side. "It's a gramophone and it plays musical recordings. An orchestra is in the room when you put this needle down."

Pettigrew peered into the cabinet. "Looks complicated."

"Here, let me show you." Flinders vigorously worked the crank and then opened the curved lid. He waved a small packet. "See, you take one of these needles and put it in the arm thus. Tighten the screw and you are ready to go." He put a large disk in the cabinet, pulled a lever, and swung the arm over it. Music played.

"That is amazing," Pettigrew agreed.

"Yes, with this you can listen to Nellie Melba as though she were singing right in front of you."

"I don't want to listen to Nellie Melba," Pettigrew said, "or eat her dessert."

"Perhaps a tango instead. And speaking of tango . . ." Flinders put on another record. "Listen to this."

Pettigrew listened. "That sounds terrible."

"Nonsense. This piece is famous. 'La Cumparsita'—'The Little Procession'—and you can dance to it. They played it in Cairo."

"Ah, at the American bar." Pettigrew chuckled. "You staggered around the floor full of bourbon and declared yourself king of the Tangueros, whatever that meant."

And then we went to Alexandria with Inji.

"Anyway, I don't know how to dance the tango."

"You must learn. Tangos are songs about the heart. You do have a heart, don't you?" Flinders laughed.

"It's not my heart—it's my feet. They don't work."

"I told you how to do it in Cairo. You just slick back your hair, put on a sour look, and walk around. I am sure that you can manage it, especially the sour look part." Flinders turned up the volume and began tangoing around the sitting room. "Watch. It's easy—just bend your knees and point your toes."

She said, "Don't drop your hip. Keep moving, effendi."

"Enough of this—now it's your turn." Flinders pushed Pettigrew through a regimen of steps. "We must improve your fledgling social skills. You never know when you might meet a beautiful woman who wants to tango." He continued prodding. "Come on—keep on moving. You are as slow as molasses."

Flinders wound the crank and put a second record on the turntable. "Try this one; it is called 'El Choclo'—'The Corncob'—and it might suit your skills better."

Pettigrew sat down, red-faced.

"Get up! What happened to the mighty swordsman?"

Lightning bursts lit the sitting room. "It's going to be a dark and stormy night." Flinders laughed, went to the window, and peered out. His shadow moved on the street below. Then his eyes traveled farther.

A tiger looked back at him from under a streetlight. Its eyes fixed on him. The streetlight reflected off its stripes. The last stanza of the Blake poem came to his mind.

Tyger Tyger burning bright,
In the forests of the night;
What immortal hand or eye,
Dare frame thy fearful symmetry?

Yes, what immortal hand or eye dare frame what I have seen?
Flinders blinked; the tiger was gone.
My imagination runs wild.
The tango's rhythms brought his mind back to the sitting room.
"Back to work, Thomas." Flinders laughed. "The pampas calls. Perhaps we should take up Spanish lessons."
"Spanish, is it?" Pettigrew said. "What happened to the acting lessons?"
"Good idea. Now that I think of it, I must have a whip and a broad hat around here somewhere."
Pettigrew groaned. "Not Hollywood again."
"Hollywood in the rain."
"What do you mean, 'Hollywood in the rain?'"
The young lovers stood in the rain.
"Yes, we can travel to Hollywood," Flinders said. "We can sail on a magnificent ocean liner."
"A magnificent ocean liner?" Pettigrew smiled. "First you wanted to sail on the Titanic, and now you propose to go on another liner. Have you forgotten that the Titanic sunk? Where will this ill-considered seagoing urge end?"
Flinders produced an owlish grin. "Who knows, my friend. Who knows?" He looked out the window once more and thought, *If a passerby on Baker Street looked up, he would have seen two figures that moved*

behind white curtains. Flinders opened the window and looked down, his hands resting on the sill. *Our outlines would be traced on the slick cobbles below.*

But there was no movement, no passersby. He saw that the street below was empty. A line of streetlights haloed yellow and alone in the rain. Gusts flurried and swept across the cobbles in sheets. Damp air caressed his face; drops spattered on his fingers. The earthy smell of rain drifted up from below.

Thunder rumbled.

Tango music echoed down the dark and empty street. Flinders listened to its melody. The melody was old, about lost love and sad memories. Then the bandoneon took up a new melody, a brighter one that ended on a note of hope. Music soared down the windy street; its theme swelled in the rain.

Flinders closed the window.

About the Author

John Amos holds a PhD from the University of California at Berkeley and a JD from the Monterey College of Law. He has taught at the university level for twenty-five years. His academic publications include two books, *Arab-Israeli Military/Political Relations* and *Palestinian Resistance*, as well as numerous articles in major academic journals. He is also a coeditor of *Gulf Security into the 1980s*. His fiction works include *The Student* (2022), *The Cleopatra Caper* (2023), and *The Case of the Stolen Goddess* (2024). He has lived and studied in the Middle East, most notably in Egypt, Lebanon, Libya, and Türkiye. He currently practices law.

Printed in Dunstable, United Kingdom

26/8/25